Death of a Dude

Death of a Dude

A NERO WOLFE NOVEL

Rex Stout

NEW YORK / THE VIKING PRESS

c1969 179p.

00B8106

First published in 1969 by The Viking Press, Inc.
625 Madison Avenue, New York, N.Y. 10022

Published simultaneously in Canada by
The Macmillan Company of Canada Limited

Printed in the United States of America

Death of a Dude

I

I BEGAN IT "NW" and signed it "AG" not to be different, but from habit. Nearly all of my written communications to Nero Wolfe over the years had been on a sheet of a memo pad, for Fritz to take up to his room on his breakfast tray, or put by me on his desk when he was upstairs in bed and I had returned from an evening errand. They had all begun "NW" and ended "AG" so this did too, though it wasn't scribbled. It was typed on an Underwood on a table in a corner of the big room in Lily Rowan's cabin in a corner of her ranch, and it was in the airmail envelope I poked through the slot in the post office in Timberburg, the county seat, that Saturday morning—on a letterhead that had *Bar JR Ranch, Lame Horse, Montana* in big type across the top. Not as elegant as the one with her New York penthouse address. Below, it said:

Friday 8:13 pm
August 2, 1968

NW:

It's a real mess here and I'm stuck. I didn't go into details on the phone Monday because someone at the exchange might be cooperating with the sheriff or the county attorney (in New York he would be district attorney), or there might even be a tap on Miss Rowan's line. Modern science certainly gets around.

Since you never forget anything or anybody you remember Harvey Greve, who once told you there in the office that he had bought a lot of livestock, horses and cattle and calves, for Roger Dunning, which helped do for Dunning. I believe I have mentioned that he has been running Miss Rowan's ranch for the last four years, and he still is—or was until six days ago, last Saturday, when he was charged with murder and parked in the cooler—namely the county jail. A dude named Philip Brodell had been shot in the back and then in the front while he was picking huckleberries. As I have told you, these mountain huckleberries are different. This time I'll try to bring you some.

Miss Rowan and I have decided that Harvey didn't do it, and I'm stuck. If it had been plain and simple that he did it I would have been back there to keep your desk dusted when I was supposed to, day before yesterday. Miss Rowan has hired a lawyer from Helena with a reputation that stretches from the Continental Divide to the Little Missouri, and it would be his problem. But I suspect he doesn't see it as we do. His head's on it, but I don't think his heart's in it. Mine is, and one will get you fifty that Harvey's clean. So you see how it is, I've got a job. Even if I had no obligation to Miss Rowan as her guest and an old friend, I've known Harvey Greve too long and too well to bow out and leave him in a squeeze.

Of course from July 31, day before yesterday, I'm on leave of absence without pay. I hope to be back soon, but as it stands now I have no suggestions for a replacement for Harvey in the jug, and it looks like—excuse it, as if—there'll have to be one with good credentials. If you want to have Saul or Orrie at my desk, my strictly personal things are up in my room, so all my secrets are safe. Television here is often a bust, and I have got to be back in time for the World Series. Give Theodore my regards and tell Fritz my first thought every morning is him—the breakfast in his kitchen I'm missing. In these parts the two favorite nicknames for pancakes are torture disks and gut plasters.

AG

When he got it, probably Monday, he would lean back and glare at my chair for a good ten minutes.

As I left the post office I took a look at my shopping list. The population of Timberburg was only 7463, but it was the biggest batch between Helena and Great Falls, and its customers covered a lot of territory—from the Fishtail River, where the hills graduated into mountains, east to where the range got so flat you could see a coyote two miles off. So in about an hour I got everything on my list, with four stops on the main drag and two on side streets. The items:

Big Six Mix pipe tobacco for Mel Fox. With Harvey in the coop he was too busy at the ranch to go shopping.

Fly swatters for Pete Ingalls. He never raised his foot to the stirrup without one dangling from his saddle horn, for horse flies.

Typewriter ribbon for the Underwood.

Tube of toothpaste and a belt, for me personally. My best belt had got chewed by a porcupine when I—but that's a long story.

A magnifying glass and a notebook that would go in my hip pocket, for me professionally. On a job in New York I never go on an errand without those two articles, and I was on a job now. Probably I wouldn't have any use for them, but a habit is a habit. Psychology.

My last stop was the public library, to consult a book that probably wouldn't be there, but it was—*Who's Who in America*. Not the latest, 1968-1969, but the 1966-1967 was good enough. There was no entry for Philip Brodell, and there never would be since he was now a corpse, but his father, Edward Ellis Brodell, had about a third of a column. I knew he was still alive, having exchanged some words with him a week ago, when he had come to gather facts and raise some hell and get his son's body to take home. Born in St. Louis in 1907, he had done all right and was now the owner and publisher of the St. Louis *Star-Bulletin*. *Who's Who* had no information about who was going to kill his son.

With all my purchases in the big paper bag I had requested for the fly swatters, I wasn't much encumbered when I entered the Continental Café at a quarter past noon, sent my eyes around, spotted an attractive female in an olive-green shirt and dark green slacks at a table in the rear, and headed for her. When I got there and pulled a chair back she said, "Either you're pretty fast or you didn't finish your list."

"Got everything." I sat and put the bag on the floor. "I may not be fast but I'm lucky." I tipped my head at her martini glass. "Carson's?"

"No. They haven't got any. You can't tell me gins are all alike. There's split-pea soup."

That was good news because his split-pea soup was the one dish the Continental cook had a right to be proud of. A waitress came and took our order for two double bowls of soup, plenty of crackers, one milk, and one coffee, and while we were waiting for it I fished in the bag for the belt and the magnifying glass to show Lily that Timberburg was as good as New York when you needed things.

The soup was up to expectations. When our bowls were nearly empty and the crackers low I said, "I not only finished up my list, I dug up some facts. At the library in *Who's Who*. Philip Brodell's father's father's name was Amos. His father is a member of three clubs, and his father's wife's maiden name was Mitchell. That's a break. Real progress."

"Congratulations." She took a cracker. "Let's go and tell Jessup. You're the doctor, but how could *Who's Who* possibly have helped?"

"It couldn't. But when you're up a stump you always try things that can't help and about once a year one does." I swallowed the last spoonful of soup. "I've got to say something."

"Good. Like?"

"Like it is. Look, Lily. I'm a good investigator with a lot of experience. But this is the sixth day since Harvey was charged and I have got nowhere. Not a glimmer of a lead. I may be only half as smart as I think I am, but also I'm handicapped. I don't belong here. I'm a dude. I'm all right for things like packing in or fishing or a game of pinochle or even a dance at the hall, but this is murder, and I'm a dude. Hell, I've been out here a lot, and I've known Mel Fox for years, and even he has gone cagey on me. They all have. I'm a goddam dude. There must be private detectives in Helena, and there may be a good one. A native. Dawson would know."

She put her coffee cup down. "You're suggesting that I hire a native to help you."

"Not to help me. If he's any good he wouldn't help *me*. He would just go to work."

"Oh." Her blue eyes widened and fastened on me. "You're checking out."

"I am not. In the letter I just mailed to Mr. Wolfe I said I hoped to be back for the World Series. I'm staying and making motions, but damn it, I'm handicapped. I'm only suggesting that maybe you should ask Dawson."

"Escamillo." Her eyes had relaxed and were smiling. "Now really. Aren't you the second-best detective in the world?"

"Oh, sure. In *my* world, but this isn't it. Even Dawson, haven't you noticed? You've paid him a ten-grand retainer, but how does he take me? You must have noticed."

She nodded. "It's one of the milder forms of xenophobia. You're a dude, and I'm a dudine."

"You own a ranch. That's different."

"Well." She picked up her coffee cup, looked in it, decided it was too cool, and put it down. "It's too bad Harvey can't be bailed out, but Mel can handle it—for a while. How much time have we got?"

"Until Harvey's tried and convicted, apparently two or three months, from what Jessup says."

"And it's two months to the World Series. You know, Archie, what I think of you personally has nothing to do with this. Not only are you a better detective than any native would be, but also you know darned well Harvey didn't shoot a man in the back. But after a week or two of nosing around, the native would probably think he did. Dawson does. Admit I'm right."

"You're always right sometimes."

"Then may I have some hot coffee?"

My milk glass was empty, so I had coffee too. When we had finished it and I had paid the check, we left, and as we made our way through the clutter of tables and chairs about twenty pairs of eyes followed us, and about twenty other pairs pretended not to. Monroe County was pretty worked up about the murder of Philip Brodell. Its basic attitude to dudes was no help in bringing on the brotherhood of man, but after all, they brought a lot of dough to Montana and left it there, and shooting them when they were picking huckleberries was not to be encouraged. So the eyes at Lily and me weren't very friendly; it was her ranch boss that had pulled the trigger. So it looked to them.

At the parking lot behind the café I put my bag in the back of Lily's station wagon, among the items she had had on her list, before I got in behind the wheel. She was sitting straight so her back wouldn't touch the seat back, which the slanting August sun had been trying to fry. My side was okay. I backed out from the slot. On a list of the differences between Lily and me it would be near the top that I park so I won't have to back out when I leave and she doesn't.

It was only two short blocks to the Presto gas station, where I turned in and stopped at the pump. The gauge said half full and the gas in the tank at the ranch cost nine cents less per gallon, but I wanted Lily to have a look at a person named Gilbert Haight who might be there. He was—a lanky loose-limbed kid whose long neck helped to make up his six feet—but he was wiping the windshield of another car, and Lily had to twist around to get focused on him as I told the other attendant to fill it up with Special. But when the other car rolled off, the kid stood looking at us for half a minute and then walked over to my open window and said, "Nice morning."

Actually he didn't say, "Nice morning"; he said, "Nice mahrnin'." But I'm not going to try to give you the native lingo, at least not often. I only want to report what happened, and that would complicate it too much and slow me down.

I agreed that it was a nice mahrnin', to be polite, though it was more than an hour past noon, and he said, "My dad told me not to talk to you."

I nodded. "Yeah, he would." His dad was Morley Haight, the county sheriff. "He has practically told *me* not to talk to anybody, but I can't break the habit, and anyway it's how I make a living."

"Uhuh. Fuzz."

Television and radio certainly spread words around. "Not me," I said. "Your dad is fuzz, but I'm private. If I asked you how you spent the day Thursday a week ago, you could say it was none of my business. When your father asked me I told him."

"So I heard." His eyes went to Lily and came back to me.

"You've been asking around about me. I'd just as soon save you some trouble."

"I'd appreciate that."

"I didn't kill that skunk."

"Good. That's what I wanted to know. That narrows it down."

"It's a insult. Look at it." He ignored his colleague, who had filled my order and was there behind his elbow. "The first shot, from behind, got his shoulder and turned him around. The second shot, from in front, got him in the throat and broke his neck and killed him. Look at that. It's a insult. I have never used more than one cartridge for a deer. Ask anybody. I can take a popgun and slice off the head of a snake at thirty yards. I can do it every time. My dad told me not to talk to you, but I wanted you to know *that*."

He turned and went, toward a car that was stopping at the other pump. His colleague took a step and said, "Two-sixty-three," and I reached for my wallet.

When we were under way again, heading northeast, I asked Lily, "Well?"

"I pass," she said. "I wanted to have a look at him, that's all right, but you told me once that it's stupid to suppose looking at a man will help you decide if he's a murderer. I don't want to be stupid and I pass. But what he said? That it's an insult?"

"Oh, that." I bore right at a fork. "He can shoot all right. Three people have told me so. And any damn fool knows that if you're going to plug a man, not just hurt him, kill him, you don't go for his shoulder. Or his neck either. But he may also be sharp. He might have figured it that everybody knew he was a good shot, so he made it look as if he wasn't. He had had plenty of time to think it over."

She considered that for a couple of miles and then asked,

"Are you sure he knew that Brodell had—that he was the father of her baby?"

"Hell, everybody in Lame Horse knew it. And beyond. Of course they also knew that Gil Haight was set on her. Last Tuesday—no, Wednesday—he told a man that he still wanted to marry her and was going to."

"That's love for you. The sharp right is just ahead."

I said I knew it.

The twenty-four miles from Timberburg to Lame Horse was all blacktop except for two short stretches—one where it dived down into a deep gully and up again, and one where winters pushed so much rock through and around that they had quit trying to keep it surfaced. For the first few miles out of Timberburg there were some trees and bushes, then broken range for the rest of the way.

The population of Lame Horse was 160, give or take a dozen. The blacktop stopped right in front of Vawter's General Store, but the road went on, curving left a little ahead. Having been to Timberburg, we needed nothing at Vawter's, so we didn't stop. From there it was 2.8 miles to the turnoff to Lily's ranch, and another 300 yards to the turnoff to her cabin. In that three miles you climbed nearly 2000 feet. To get to the ranch buildings you crossed a bridge over Berry Creek, but from there the creek took a swing to make a big loop, and the cabin was in the loop, only a few hundred yards inside the ranch boundary. To get to the ranch buildings on foot from the cabin you had to cross the creek, either by the bridge or, much shorter, by fording just outside the cabin. In August there was a spot where it could be done by stone-stepping. A better name for it would be boulder-bouncing.

My favorite spot on earth is only a seven-minute walk from where I live, Nero Wolfe's house on West 35th Street: Herald Square, where you can see more different kinds of people in ten minutes than anywhere else I know of. One day I saw the top cock of the Mafia step back to let a Sunday-school teacher from Iowa go first through the revolving door of the world's largest department store. If you ask how I knew who they were, I didn't, but that's what they looked like. But for anyone who is fed up with people and noise, the favorite spot could be Lily Rowan's cabin clearing. I admit there is a little noise, Berry Creek making a fuss about the rocks that won't move, but after a couple of days you hear it only when you want to. The big firs start farther up, but there are plenty of trees right there, mostly lodgepole pine, and downstream is Beaver Meadow; and just upstream, where the creek swings around again to the north, is a cliff of solid rock you can't see the top of from this side of the creek. If you need exercise and want to throw stones at gophers it's only a three-minute walk down the lane to the road.

The cabin is logs of course, and is all on one level. Crossing a stone-paved terrace with a roof, you enter a room 34 by 52, with a 10-foot fireplace at the rear, and for living that's it. For privacy or sleeping, there are two doors at the right, one to Lily's room and the other to a guest room. A door at the left leads to a long hall, and when you take it, first comes a big kitchen, then Mimi's room, then a big store-room, and then three guest rooms. There are six baths, complete with tubs and showers. A very nice little cabin. Except for the beds, the furniture you sit on is nearly all wicker. The rugs in all rooms are Red Indian, and on the walls, instead of pictures, are Indian blankets and rugs. Three of them in the big room are genuine bayetas. There is just one picture on view anywhere, a framed photograph of Lily's father and mother on the piano—one of the few things she carts back and forth from New York.

Some of the items Lily had got at Timberburg that morning were for the kitchen and storeroom, and with them we saved steps by skirting the terrace to a door direct to the hall. There was no offer of help from the dark-eyed beauty with a pointed chin who was on a chair in the sun off the edge of the terrace. Since her halter and shorts didn't total more than three square feet, there was a lot of smooth tan skin showing, with her bare legs out straight to the foot extension. She had greeted us with a graceful wave as we got out of the car. Back from the deliveries to the kitchen and storeroom, Lily took the few things that were left, and I backed the car into a space among the lodgepoles and got my paper bag. Lily had stopped by Diana's chair to give her one of the packages.

Her name was Diana Kadany. A house guest at Lily's cabin might be anyone from a tired-out social worker to a famous composer of the kind of music I can get along without. That year there were three, counting me, which was par. Discussing Diana Kadany one day when we were up at the second pool getting trout for supper, I had guessed she was twenty-two and Lily had guessed twenty-five. She had made a sort of a hit the previous winter in an off-Broadway play entitled *Not Me You Don't,* the kind of play that would go fine with music by that famous composer I mentioned, and she had been invited to Montana only because Lily, having helped stake the play, was curious about her. Of course that was risky, taking on a question mark for a month, but it hadn't been too bad. It was only a minor nuisance that she practiced being seductive with any male who happened to be handy. Of course Wade Worthy and I were the handiest.

As I crossed the big room to the door to my room, the one at the far right, Wade Worthy was at the table in the corner, banging away on the Underwood. He was the other guest, but a special kind of guest. He was doing a job. For two years Lily had collected material about her father, and when there was about half a ton of it she had started looking for someone to write the book, thinking that with the help of a friend of hers who was an editor at the Parthenon Press it might take a week. It had taken nearly three months. Of the first twenty-two professional authors considered, three were busy writing books, four were getting ready to, two were in hospitals, one was too mad about Vietnam to talk about anything else, three were out of the country, one was experimenting with LSD, two were Republicans and wouldn't write the kind of book Lily had in mind about a Tammany Hall man who had made a pile building sewers and laying pavements, one wanted a year to decide, three said they weren't interested without giving a reason, one was trying to make up his mind whether to switch to fiction, and one was drunk.

Finally, in May, Lily and the editor had tagged Wade Worthy. According to the editor, no one in the literary world had ever heard of him until three years ago, when his biography of Abbott Lawrence Lowell had been published. It had done only fairly well, but his second book, about Heywood Broun, with the title *The Head and the Heart,* had nearly made the best-seller list. Lily's offer of a fat advance, with only half to be deducted from royalties—which the editor strongly disapproved—had appealed to him, and there he was at the typewriter, working on the outline. The title was to be *A Stripe of the Tiger: the Life and Work of James Gilmore Rowan.* Lily was hoping as many copies of it would be sold as there were steers branded Bar JR. The JR stood for James Rowan.

In my room I emptied the bag, put the belt around my middle, the toothpaste in the bathroom, and the notebook and magnifying glass in my pockets, went out again with the other three items, and detoured to the corner in the big room to give Wade Worthy the typewriter ribbon. Outside, Lily

was still with Diana Kadany. I told her I'd take the car because I might go on to Lame Horse or Farnham's, and she
told me not to be late for supper. I got in the car, rolled down
the lane to the road, turned left and left again in a sixth of a
mile at the turnoff, crossed the bridge over Berry Creek,
went through an open gate which was usually shut, passed
corrals and two barns and a bunkhouse—which Pete Ingalls called the dorm—and stopped at the edge of a big
square of dusty gravel with a tree in the middle, in front of
Harvey Greve's house.

II

I COULD TELL you a lot about the Bar JR Ranch—how many acres, how many head, the trial and error with alfalfa that had been mostly error, the fence problem, the bookkeeping complications, the open-range question, and so on—but that has nothing to do with a dead dude and how to get Harvey back where he belonged. Irrelevant and immaterial. But the person who appeared inside the screen door as I got out of the car was relevant. As I approached she opened the door and I went in.

I have never met a nineteen-year-old boy who gave me the impression that he knew things I wouldn't understand, but three girls around that age have, and little Alma Greve was one of them. Don't ask me if it was the deep-set brown eyes that seldom opened wide, or the curve of her lips that seemed to be starting a smile but never made it, or what, because I don't know. When I had mentioned it to Lily a couple of years back she had said, "Oh, come on. It's not her, it's you. Every pretty girl a man sees, either she's a mystery he could learn from, or she's an innocent he could—uh—edify. Either way, he's always wrong. Of course with you she's seldom a mystery because what don't you understand?"

I had grabbed a clump of paintbrush and thrown it at her.

I asked Alma who was around, and she said her mother was taking a nap and the baby was asleep. She asked me if her mother had asked me to get fly swatters, and I said no, they were for Pete.

"Maybe we could sit and talk a little," I said.

Her head was tilted back because her eyes were nine inches lower than mine. "I told you," she said, "I'm talked out. But all right."

She turned and I followed her into what they called the front room, but they could have called it the trophy room. Harvey and Carol, his wife, had formerly both been rodeo stars, and the walls were covered with pictures—him bull-dogging steers and both of them riding broncs and tying calves. Also there were displays of ribbons they had won, and medals, and in a glass case on a table was a big silver cup Harvey had got one year at Calgary, with his name engraved on it. Alma went to a couch by the fireplace and sat with her legs crossed, and I took a nearby chair. Her skirt was mini—she never wore shorts—but her legs were no match for Diana's, in either length or caliber. There was nothing wrong with what there was of them.

"You look all right," I said. "You're getting your sleep."

She nodded. "Go right ahead. Ride me. I'm saddle-broke."

"You chew the bit." I regarded her. "Look, Alma. I love you dearly, we all love you, but can't you get it in your head that someone is going to take the rap for killing Philip Brodell, and it's going to be your father unless we produce a miracle?"

"This is Montana," she said.

"Yeah. The Treasure State. Gold and silver."

"My father won't take any rap. This is Montana. They'll acquit him."

"Who told you that?"

"Nobody had to tell me. I was born here."

"But too late. Fifty years ago, or even less, a Montana

jury might not convict a man who had shot a man who had
seduced his daughter. But not today, not even if you go on
the stand with the baby in your arms and say you're glad he
killed him. I've decided to tell you exactly what I think. I
think you have an idea about who did kill him, maybe even
actual knowledge, and you don't want *him* to take the rap,
and you think your father won't have to because they won't
convict him. You've admitted you're glad somebody killed
him."

"I didn't say that."

"Nuts. I can repeat it verbatim, all of it. You're glad he's
dead."

"All right, I am."

"And you don't want anybody to get tagged for it. For instance, suppose you have reason to think that Gil Haight
killed him. Gil says he was in Timberburg all day that
Thursday, he has told several people that, but suppose you
know he wasn't? Suppose he was here that day, and he said
things, and from here it's only a couple of miles to where
Brodell was shot, and he had a gun in his car. But you're sav-
ing it because you think your father will be acquitted, and
you also think that if he isn't, if he's convicted of first-degree
murder and sent up, you could get him out by telling *then*
what you know. Well, you couldn't, for several reasons, the
best one being that nobody would believe you. But if you
tell me now I can take it from there and we'll see what happens. Gil Haight would stand as good a chance as your father does. He's a local boy with a clean record, and he was
hoping to marry you, and when the man who had seduced
you last summer showed up again this summer he went off
his nut. At least as good a chance as your father, maybe
better."

There was a sound from the other side of an open door,
not the one to the hall, which could have been a baby turning

over and kicking the crib, and she turned her head. Silence, and she returned to me. "Gil wasn't here that day," she said.

"I didn't say he was, I was only supposing. There are other possibilities. Someone might have killed him for some other reason, nothing to do with you. If so, the reason was probably a carry-over from last year, because Brodell had only been here three days this year. If it was something from last year, for instance some kind of trouble with Farnham, he might have mentioned it to you. When a man gets close enough with a woman to make a baby he might mention anything. Damn it, if you would drop your cockeyed idea that your father will be acquitted, and put your mind on it, you might give me a start."

Her lips almost made the smile. "You think my mind's not on it?"

"Your feelings are on it, but your mind, no."

"Certainly my mind's on it." She uncrossed her legs and put her hands on her knees. "Listen, Archie. I've told you ten times, I think my father killed him."

"And I've told you ten times, you *can't*. I don't believe it. You're not a halfwit, and you'd have to be one to live with him nineteen years and not—"

A voice said, "She's not a halfwit, she's just a dope."

Carol was there in the doorway. "My daughter," she said, "the only one I've got, and what a piece of luck that was." She was coming. "You might as well quit on her. I have." She looked down at Alma. "Please go and milk a mule or something. I want to talk with Archie."

Alma stayed put. "He said he wanted to talk with me. I don't want to talk at all. What's the use?"

"None at all." Carol sat, on the couch, at arm's length from Alma. From the neck down she was close to frowzy, with a rumpled shirt and old brown work pants, and socks but no shoes, but her face could still have been the face of a cowgirl in her twenties except for the wrinkles around the sharp brown eyes. The eyes focused on me. "I guess you haven't scared up any dust or you wouldn't be here."

"Right. You saw Harvey yesterday?"

She nodded. "For half an hour. That's all Morley Haight would allow. I've known that man— Someone ought to pin his ears back. Maybe me."

"I'll help. Anything from Harvey?"

"No. Nothing but more of the same."

I shook my head. "I want to ask you something. I told Lily today that she might ask Dawson if there's a good private detective in Helena. Product of Montana. People might tell him things they won't tell me. What do you think?"

"That's funny," she said.

"Funny how?"

"Two people have had the same idea. Flora and a friend of mine you don't know. I asked Harvey yesterday what he thought, and he said no. He said there wouldn't be any detective in Helena half as good as you, and anyway Dawson thinks he shot that man, and so would anybody he got. Everyone around here does, you know that."

"Not everyone. Not the man that shot him. Okay, skip it for now. You said you want to talk."

She looked at her daughter. "You're not my little heifer now, you've dropped a calf. I can't shoo you out." She stood up and said to me, "If you will please, we'll go outdoors."

Alma rose, thought she was going to say something but decided not to, headed for the door, and was gone. When she was out Carol went and shut the door, came back and sat at the end of the couch, closer to me, and said, "You could be right about her, but maybe not. She *ought* to know her father, but maybe she doesn't because he *is* her father. I can remember, I thought I knew mine when I was nineteen, but I didn't. I didn't find out until— To hell with it, that trail's grown over. What I wanted to tell you, I had an idea, but I'm not saying it's any good."

"Even a bad idea would be welcome."

"It's that couple at Bill Farnham's. Not the pair from Denver, that doctor and his wife from Seattle. Didn't I hear you say he's a doctor?"

I nodded. "Robert C. Amory, M.D., and his wife Beatrice."

"How old are they?"

"Oh, around forty."

"What's she like?"

"Five feet six, hundred and twenty pounds. Fairly lookable. Hair dyed red, and I doubt if she brought a supply along. Tries to pretend she likes it here, but she came only because he needed to get away from the grind and he loves to ride and fish."

"What's he like? If that Brodell laid her and he found out, what would he do?"

"Brodell would have had to move fast. He had only been here three days."

"We've got a bull that doesn't even need one day."

"Yeah, I've met that bull, as you know. Brodell wasn't that type, but I admit it's possible. I also admit that I had that idea Tuesday, four days ago, and I asked some questions that Bill Farnham resented. I got a couple of facts that didn't hurt, but they didn't prove anything. One, Dr. Amory has no alibi for that Thursday afternoon because he was upriver alone, and two, he can't shoot worth a damn. I was hoping for a fact with juice in it, for instance that he had taken a gun along that day in case he met a bear, but Farnham said no."

"Of couse he said no. He wouldn't want one of his dudes corralled for murder."

"Sure. I'm just telling you what he said. As for believing

him, I believe damn little of what a lot of people have told me the last six days. Even you. You told me day before yesterday that you never saw Philip Brodell. Do I have to believe that?"

"It's true."

"He was here six weeks last summer. Just four miles from this spot."

"It might have been four hundred miles. I wish it was. Bill Farnham has a dude ranch and this is a working ranch, and Harvey and Bill have had some words, you know that. You were here the time a few cattle found a bad spot in the fence and made it to the woods and one of his dudes shot a steer. We don't visit. The only way I know Alma met that Brodell at a dance at the hall, that's what she told me. She never mentioned him once last year, but if you don't want to believe I never saw him it's your rope. Are you quitting on that doctor?"

"I'm not quitting on anybody. The only reason you're not on the list is that it wouldn't help any to tie it on you. Trading you for Harvey would be no improvement, even if you *would* shoot a man in the back."

"If I did I wouldn't hit him in the shoulder."

"Unless you wanted to." Our eyes were meeting. "I don't think I've asked you, have I?"

"Asked me what?"

"If you shot him."

"Nope. Twice. You haven't asked me and I didn't shoot him. You must be awful hard up for a meld."

"Certainly I am. You know I am. But I'm not just talking to hear myself. Let's see if we agree on a couple of points— three points. First, you're not Harvey, you're you, and you're a woman, and you *might* shoot a man in the back. Second, you're a good shot, and the bullet would go within half an inch of where you wanted it."

"Not half an inch. It would go *where* I wanted it."

"Okay. Now the third point. A lot of people, probably including Haight and Jessup, are saying that Harvey got him in the shoulder to turn him around, and then in the neck because everyone knows he can shoot and he wanted it to look as if the man who did it *couldn't* shoot. The trouble with that is that Harvey simply hasn't got that kind of a dodge in him. Granting that he would shoot him in the back at all, which I don't, it would never enter his mind to kink it like that. But your mind is different. It would enter *your* mind. Do you agree on the three points?"

A corner of her mouth was twisted up. "Lily," she said.

"What about Lily?"

"She thinks I shot him, huh?"

"If she does she hasn't said so. This is just you and me. Even if Lily thinks that and has told me so, I do my own thinking. Do we agree on the three points?"

The corner of her mouth stayed up. "Suppose I say yes, then what? You said yourself that trading me for Harvey would be no improvement. Maybe you didn't mean it?"

"Certainly I meant it. It's obvious. But I asked Alma to do some supposing, and now I ask you to do some. Suppose you shot him, but I go on as if you didn't. In that case, where am I? I can't dig up evidence that would pin it on somebody else, because there isn't any. I'm hog-tied, and anything and everything I do will be crap. But if I knew you shot him maybe I could do something that wouldn't be crap. I've had some experience helping with tough problems, and I have been known to come up with an idea now and then. Strictly between you and me, let's talk turkey."

Her look was a squint, the squint that had made the wrinkles. She said, just stating a fact, "So you do think I shot him."

"I do not. I only realize it's possible. Alma's saying you

were both here all afternoon that day doesn't prove anything, because of course she would say that. I admit you
would be a damn fool to tell me you shot him if there was
the slightest chance that I would pass it on, and I guess you
don't know me well enough to be dead sure of me. There
are a few people in New York who do, but nobody here does
except maybe Harvey. As you know, I can't get to him. If
you tell him that I'll give you my word that I'll pass it on to
no one, not even Lily, no matter what happens, I think he
would tell you to open up."

"So you're *sure* I shot him."

"Damn it, I am not! But I'm hobbled and I've got to know.
Don't you see the fix I'm in?"

"Yeah. I see. Well . . ." She looked around. "We haven't
got a Bible." She got up and sent her eyes around again, and
crossed to a corner where a saddle, not much used, hung on
a wooden peg. "You know about this saddle," she said.

I nodded. "A hand-made Quantrell, with silver stirrups
and rivets and studs, and you won it at Pendleton in nineteen
forty-seven."

"I sure did. My biggest day, that was." She cupped her
palm over the horn and aimed her eyes at me. "If I shot that
Brodell toad may this saddle mold up and rot and stink and
get maggots, so help me God." She turned to pat the cantle
and back to me. "Is that good enough?"

"I wouldn't ask for any better." I was on my feet. "All
right, you're out, we cross you off, and it's a job. Tell Harvey
I hope I'm as good as he thinks I am. I'll need to be." I
pointed. "The tobacco is for Mel and the fly swatters are for
Pete. I won't wait until they come in because I want to take
a look at something. You heard what I said to Alma?"

"Most of it."

"She was here with you that afternoon? All of it?"

"I've told you, yes."

"And Gil Haight wasn't here?"

"I've told you, no."

I started out, turned, and said, "Still on the saddle."

"It's still yes and no," she said.

III

IF THE WAY I spent the next three hours seems not very brilliant, I haven't made it clear enough how tough the situation was. I went to have a look at the scene of the crime.

The road from Lame Horse to the turnoffs to the Bar JR Ranch and Lily's cabin doesn't stop there. It keeps going for three more miles and stops for good at the Fishtail River, and there, on the right, is Bill Farnham's dude ranch. It's small compared with some, and deluxe compared with almost any—not counting Lily's cabin. Farnham's limit is six dudes at a time, and a few days before Brodell was killed a guy from Spokane had broken an arm and gone home, so now there were only four—Dr. and Mrs. Amory and the pair from Denver. There was no Mrs. Farnham, and for help there was a female cook, a girl who did the house chores, and two wranglers named Bert Magee and Sam Peacock. There were no dude cabins and only one building of any size, a combo of log and frame with ells in the middle and at the ends, taking about half an acre. The barn and corrals were away from the river, beyond a stand of jack pine.

When I stopped the car between a couple of big firs and got out there was no one in sight, and around at the river side of the house, where there were chairs and tables on a carpet of needles, still no one; but when I crossed to the screen door and sang out, "Anybody home?" a voice told me to come in and I entered. The room was about half the size of the big room in Lily's cabin, and on a rug in the middle of it a woman with red hair was stretched out on her back with her head propped on a stack of cushions. As I approached she tossed a magazine aside, said, "I recognized your voice," and patted her mouth for a yawn.

I stopped a polite four paces short and said I hoped I hadn't disturbed a nap. She said no, she did her sleeping at night, and added, "Don't mind it, please, I'm too lazy to pull down my skirt. I hate pants." She patted a yawn. "If you didn't come to see me you're out of luck. They all left at dawn to ford the river and ride up the mountain to try to see some elk, and there's no telling when they'll get back. Are you still—uh, well—trying to get your friend out of jail?"

"Just for something to do. Shall I pull the skirt down?"

"Don't bother. If you came to see me I can't imagine what for, but here I am."

I smiled down at her to show I appreciated the chitchat. "Actually, Mrs. Amory, I didn't come to see anyone. I only wanted to tell Bill that I'm leaving the car here to go for a look at Blue Grouse Ridge. If he comes before I do, tell him, will you?"

"Of course, but he won't." She brushed a strand of the red hair back from her temples. "That's where it happened, isn't it?"

I said yes and turned to go, but turned back to her voice. "I guess you know I'm the only one here that's rooting for you. They all think he—I forget his name—"

"Greve. Harvey Greve."

She nodded. "They all think he did it. I know an intelligent man when I see one, and I think you're one, and I bet you know what you're doing. Good luck."

I thanked her and went.

I knew Blue Grouse Ridge because it was the best place around for huckleberries, and Lily and I had been there often—sometimes for berries and sometimes for young blue grouse which, about ten weeks old and grubbed almost exclusively on berries, were as good eating as anything Fritz had ever served. Of course it was against the law to take them, so of course we didn't overdo it. We had gone to the ridge, for berries, not blue grouse, just two days before Brodell was killed, with Diana Kadany and Wade Worthy.

I could have got there cross-country from the Bar JR or the cabin, but it was twice as far and rough going part of the way. From Farnham's it was only a mile or so with no hard climbing. Beyond the barn and corrals there was a close stand of firs on a down slope with no windfalls, and thick soft duff underfoot, then a rocky stretch I had to zigzag through, and then a big field of bear grass up the slope of the ridge. The bear grass, dry and tough in August, slowed me down, trying to tangle my legs. When I was through it, fifty yards or so short of the crest, I turned left and went parallel with the ridge, looking for signs—trampling of feet or brush cleared, anything. I am no mountain tracker, but certainly there would be something that would show even a dude where enough men had come to pack out a two-legged carcass. But the first sign that placed it for me was one that could have been anywhere on earth, as good on Herald Square as on Blue Grouse Ridge—blood. There was a blotch of it, or what had been left of it by the tongue of some animal, on the surface of a boulder, and a narrow ribbon of it down the boulder to the lower edge. At the upper edge of the boulder there was a big clump of berry bushes, so he had been standing there picking berries when the bullet came from behind.

Having seen the blood first, I then saw a lot of other signs which a native would probably have seen first: twigs and branches of bushes, including huckleberries, twisted and broken, rocks that had recently been moved, paintbrush trampled, and so on. Feet and hands had been busy all around, even up above the boulder, and that must have been in a search for the bullets. Having detected that, I turned to face downhill to consider the detail that I was most interested in, cover for the approach. There was nothing much within a hundred feet but berry bushes and boulders, with a scattering of paintbrush and other small stuff, but beyond there was higher growth and trees. It would have been a cinch for even a New York character like me to get within forty yards of the target, let alone a man who knew how to stalk deer and elk. But forty yards is too far to count on a hand gun, so it had been a rifle, and in the middle of a Montana summer nobody goes out with a rifle for anything with four legs, except maybe a coyote, and you don't climb Blue Grouse Ridge for a coyote.

I picked a handful of berries and went and sat on a rock. I may as well admit it, I had been ass enough to hope that a look at the scene would give me a notion of some kind that would open a crack. It hadn't and it wouldn't. This wasn't my world, and if in that jumble of outdoor stuff there was some hint of who had sneaked up on Philip Brodell and plugged him, it wasn't for me. Three hours wasted. When a chipmunk showed and darted into a clump, I picked up a pebble the size of a golf ball, and when he skipped out I threw it at him, and of course missed. And at the cabin some of my best friends were chipmunks. Pleased with nothing whatever, I headed downhill and made it back to Farnham's and the car without breaking a leg. There was no one around. It was a little after five-thirty when I arrived at the cabin, and supper was at six.

The rule was to go to supper as you were, but sweat had dried on me, so I went to my room and rinsed off and changed to a PSI shirt and brown woolen slacks. As I was brushing my hair there was a tap on the door of the little hall between Lily's room and mine and I went and opened it to her. She was still in the same green shirt and slacks, and when she saw I had changed she said, "Company coming?" and I told her where I had been, spotting the bloody boulder for her by saying it was about two hundred yards north of where she had once watched me pick a fool hen off a tree with one hand. Also I told her about my talks with Alma and Carol.

"I don't know about you," I said, "but I've bought it. I have filed her. Her hand on a Bible might not have sold me, but her hand on that saddle did."

Lily had puckered her lips. She unpuckered them and nodded. "All right, then that's settled. I wanted to try that saddle on Cat once just to see how it sat, and she wouldn't let me. You were right. If she had shot him she would have told you. But don't get the idea that you're a better judge of women than I am."

Not meaning that she had wanted to try the saddle on a bobcat or mountain lion. She had named her pinto mare Cat because of the way she had jumped a ditch the first day she rode her, three years ago.

We ate breakfast and lunch in the kitchen, on a table by the big window, and sometimes supper too, but usually the place for supper was the screened terrace on the creek side. It was more trouble because Lily brought no one but Mimi from New York and wouldn't have local help, and the table-waiting was done by us. That evening it was filets mignons, baked potatoes, spinach, and raspberry sherbet, and everything but the potatoes had come from the king-size walk-in deep freeze in the storeroom. The filets mignons had been shipped by express from Chicago, packed in dry ice. You might suppose that with all of the thousands of tons of beef on the hoof just across the creek, Lily's property, there was a better and cheaper way, but that had been tried and found wanting.

At table on the terrace Lily always sat facing the creek, which was only a dozen steps from the terrace edge, with Wade Worthy on her left and me on her right and Diana Kadany across from her. As she picked up her knife Diana said, "I had an awful thought today. Utterly awful."

Of course that was a cue. It was Wade Worthy who obliged her by taking it. I hadn't fully decided about Wade. His full-cheeked face, with a broad nose and a square chin, had an assortment of grins, and they were hard to sort out. The friendly grin looked friendly, but with it he might say something sour, and with the grin that looked sarcastic he might say something nice. The one he gave Diana now was neither of those, just polite. With it he said, "You're not a good judge of your own thoughts, no one is. Tell us and we'll vote on it."

"If I wasn't going to tell you," Diana said, "I wouldn't have mentioned it." She forked a bite of meat to her mouth and started to chew. She often did that; she might get a part in a play with an eating scene, and mixing chewing and talking needed practice. An actor can practice anywhere any time with anybody, and most of them do. "It was this," she said. "If that man hadn't been murdered, Archie wouldn't be here. He would have left three days ago. So the murderer did us a favor. You won't have to vote on that. That's an awful thought."

"We'll thank him when we know who he is," Lily said.

Diana swallowed daintily and took a bite of potato. "It's no joke, Lily. It was an awful thought, but it gave me an idea for a play. Someone could write a play about a woman who does awful things—you know, she lies, she steals, she cheats, she takes other women's husbands, she might even murder somebody. But the play would show that every time she hurts someone it helps a lot of other people. She makes some people suffer awful agonies, but she gives ten times as many people some kind of benefit. She does lots more good than she does harm. I haven't decided what the last scene would be, that would be up to whoever writes the play, but it could be a wonderful scene, utterly wonderful. Any actress would love it. I know I would."

The bite of potato was gone and another bite of meat was being chewed. She was really pretty good at it, but she had the advantage of a very attractive face. A girl with a good face has to be really messy to make you want to look somewhere else when she talks while she eats. Diana looked at Worthy and said, "You're a writer, Wade. Why couldn't you do it?"

He shook his head. "Not that kind of writer. Suggest it to Albee or Tennessee Williams. As for the murderer doing us a favor, it wasn't much of one. We've seen darned little of Archie this week." He looked at me, the friendly grin. "How's it going?"

"Fine." I swallowed food. "All I need now is a confession. Diana was there picking berries on the best and biggest bush, and he came and pushed her away and she shot him. Luckily—"

"What with?" Diana demanded.

"Don't interrupt. Luckily Wade came along with a gun, out after gophers, and he shot him first but only in the shoulder, and you asked him to let you try and he handed you the gun."

Wade pointed his knife at me. "We're not going to confess. You'll have to prove it."

"Okay. Do you know about personal congenital radiation?"

"No."

"That the personal congenital radiation of no two people is the same, like fingerprints?"

"It sounds reasonable."

"It's not only reasonable, it's scientific. It's a wonder any detective ever detected anything without modern science. I went to Blue Grouse Ridge today with a *new* Geiger counter, eight cents off the regular price, and it gave me Diana *and* you. You had both been there. All I need now—"

"Certainly we were there," Diana said with her mouth full. "You and Lily took us there! Three or four times!"

"Prove it," Lily said. "I don't remember."

"Lily! You do! You must!"

One of the difficulties about Diana was that you were never absolutely sure whether she was playing dumb or *was* dumb.

By the time we got to sherbet and coffee the evening had been discussed and settled. Evenings could be pinochle, reading books or magazines or newspapers, television, conversation, or private concerns in out rooms, or sometimes, especially Saturdays, contacts with natives. For that evening Wade suggested pinochle, but I said it would have to be three-handed because I was going to Lame Horse. They considered going along and decided not to, and after doing my share of table-clearing I went out and started the car.

Now I have a problem. If I report fully what I did the next four days and nights, from eight p.m. Saturday to eight p.m. Wednesday, you will meet dozens of people and be better acquainted with Monroe County, Montana, but you will not have gained an inch on the man or woman who shot Philip Brodell, because I didn't; and you may get fed up, as I almost did. I'll settle for one sample if you will, and the sample might as well be that Saturday evening.

Since most of the Saturday-night crowd at Lame Horse came in cars and it was only twenty-four miles to Timberburg, you might suppose they would go on to the county seat, where there was a movie house with plush seats and a bowling alley and other chances to frolic, but no. Just the opposite; Saturday night quite a few people who lived in Timberburg, as many as a hundred or more, came to Lame Horse. The attraction was a big old ramshackle frame building next to Vawter's General Store which had a sign twenty feet long at the edge of the roof, reading:

WOODROW STEPANIAN HALL OF CULTURE

That was the hall, usually called Woody's. Woody, now in his sixties, had built it some thirty years ago with money left him by his father, who had peddled anything you care to name all over that part of the state even before it was a state. All of Woody's young years had been spent in a traveling department store. At birth he had been named Theodore, for Roosevelt, but when he was ten years old his father had changed it to Woodrow, for Wilson. In 1942 Woody had considered changing it to Franklin, for another Roosevelt, but had decided there would be too many complications, including changing the sign.

First on the Saturday-night program at the hall was a movie, which started at eight o'clock and which I didn't really need, so after parking the car down the road I went to Vawter's. Inside the high-ceilinged room a hundred feet long and nearly as wide, it was obvious why I wouldn't have had to go to Timberburg except for mailing the letter and consulting *Who's Who*. A complete inventory would take several pages, so I mention only a few items such as frying pans, ten-gallon hats, five-gallon coffee pots, fishing tackle, magazines and paperbacks, guns and ammunition, groceries of all kinds, ponchos, spurs and saddles, cigars and cigarettes and tobacco, nuts and candies, hunting knives and kitchen knives, cowboy boots and rubber waders, men's

wear and women's wear, a tableload of Levi's, picture post-
cards, ballpoint pens, three shelves of drugs . . .

A dozen or so customers were scattered around, and Mort
Vawter, his wife, Mabel, and his son Johnny were busy with
them. I hadn't come to buy, or even to talk, but to listen, and
after a look around I decided that the best prospect was a
leather-skinned woman with stringy black hair who was in-
specting a display of shoes on a counter. She was Henrietta,
a halfbreed bootlegger who lived down the road, and she
knew everybody. I moseyed over and said, "Hi, Henrietta.
I bet you don't remember me."

She moved her head a little sideways to give her black
eyes a slant at me, as cautious people often do. "What you
bet?"

"Oh, a buck."

"Huh. Miss Rowan's man. Mr. Archie Goodwin." She
put a hand out palm up. "One buck."

"Huh yourself. You may not mean what you could mean,
so I'll skip it." I had my wallet out. "It's a pleasant surprise
seeing you here." I handed her a bill. "I would have thought
you'd be busy with customers Saturday evening."

She turned the bill over to see the other side. "Trick?"
She grunted and spread her fingers, and the bill fluttered
to the floor. "New trick."

"No trick." I picked up the finif and offered it. "One buck
of this is the bet. The rest is for your time answering a couple of questions I want to ask."

"I don't like questions."

"Not about you. As you know, my friend Harvey Greve
is in trouble."

She grunted. "Bad trouble."

"Very bad. You may also know I'm trying to help him."

"Everybody knows."

"Yeah. And everybody seems to think I can't, because

he killed that man. You see a lot of people and hear a lot of talk. Do they all think that?"

She pointed at the bill in my hand. "I answer and you pay? Four dollars?"

"I pay first. Take it and then answer."

She took it, looked at both sides again, poked it in a pocket in her skirt, and said, "I don't go to the court."

"Of course not. This is just a friendly talk."

"Many people say Mr. Greve killed him. Not all. Some people say you killed him."

"How many?"

"Maybe three, maybe four. You know Emmy?"

I said yes. Emmy was Emmett Lake, who rode herd at the Bar JR and was known to be one of Henrietta's best customers. "Don't tell me he says I did it."

"No. He say a man at Mr. Farnham's."

"I know he does, but he doesn't say which one. I don't suppose you'd care to tell me what you think."

"Me think? Huh."

I gave her a man-to-woman smile. "I bet you think plenty."

"What you bet?"

"I couldn't prove it. Look, Henrietta, as I said, you hear a lot of talk. He was here six weeks last year—the man who was killed. He told me he bought something from you."

"One time. With Mr. Farnham."

"Did he say anything about anybody?"

"I forget."

"But you don't forget what people have said about him this week, since he was killed. That's my most important question. I don't expect you to name anybody, only what anyone has said about him." I got a sawbuck from my wallet and kept it visible. "It might help me help Mr. Greve. Tell me what you've heard about him."

Her black eyes lowered to fix on the bill and raised again. "No," she said.

And it stayed no, though I spent ten minutes trying to budge her. I returned the sawbuck to my wallet. It wouldn't have done any good to double it or even make it a hundred; she wasn't going to risk being asked questions in the court even if I swore on ten saddles that she wouldn't have to. I left her and surveyed the field. Of the dozen or more people in view, I knew the names of all but three, but none of them was likely to spill any beans, and I went out and along to Woody's.

The hall was even bigger than Vawter's store outside, but inside it was partitioned into three sections, with the entrance at the middle section, which had shelves and counters with displays of cultural material, some of it for sale. There were phonograph records, paperbacks, reproductions of paintings and drawings, busts of great men, facsimiles of the Declaration of Independence, and a slew of miscellaneous items like the Bible in Armenian, most of them one-of-a-kind. Very few people ever bought anything there; Woody had told Lily that he took in about twenty dollars a week. His income came from the other two sections, where you had to pay to get in—the one at the left to see a movie and the one at the right to dance and mix, both Saturdays only.

When I entered, Woody was conversing with a quartet of dudes from some ranch upriver or downriver, three men and a woman, whom I had never seen before. I listened a while, looking at paperbacks, learning nothing. Woody claimed he never offered a book for sale unless he had read it, and I won't call him a liar. His opinion of dudes in general was fully as low as that of most of his fellow Montanans, but he liked Lily so he accepted me, and he left the quartet to come and ask me if Miss Rowan was coming. I told him no, she was tired and going early to bed, and she had asked me to give him her regards.

He wasn't as short as Alma Greve, but he too had to tilt his head back to me. His eyes were as black as Henrietta's, and his mop of hair was as white as the top of Chair Mountain. "I bow to her," he said. "I kiss her hand with deep respect. She is a doll. May I ask, have you made some progress?"

"No, Woody, I haven't. Are you still with us?"

"I am. Forever and a day. If Mr. Greve shot that man like a coward I am a bow-legged coyote. I have told you I had the pleasure of meeting him when he was two years old. I was sixteen. His mother bought four blankets from my father that day and two dozen handkerchiefs. You have made no progress?"

"Not a smell. Have you?"

He shook his head, slow, his lips pursed. "I must confess I haven't. Of course during the week I don't see many people. Tonight there will be much talk and I'll keep my ears open, and with some I can ask questions. You will stay?"

I said sure, that I had already asked questions of everybody who might have answers, but I would listen to the talk. A pair of dudes had entered and were approaching to speak with the famous Woody, and I went back to the paperbacks, picked one entitled *The Greek Way,* by Edith Hamilton, which I had heard mentioned by both Lily and Nero Wolfe, and went to a bench with it.

At 9:19 a man in a pink shirt, working Levi's, cowboy boots, and a yellow neck rag, arrived, opened the door at the right, and set up his equipment, supplied by Woody, just outside the door—a till and a box of door checks on a little table. The gun at his belt was for looks only; Woody always checked it to make sure it wasn't loaded. At 9:24 the musicians came—having met at Vawter's probably, at Henrietta's possibly—dressed fully as properly as the doorman, with a violin, an accordion, and a sax. Local talent. The piano, which Lily said was as good as hers, was on the platform inside. At 9:28 the first patrons showed, and at 9:33 the door at the left opened and the movie audience poured out, most of them across to the other door; and the fun started. The next four hours was what brought people of all ages from Timberburg, and both natives and dudes from as far away as Flat Bank. When the rush at the door had let up a little I paid my two bucks and went in. The band was playing "Horsey, Keep Your Tail Up," and fifty couples were already on the floor, twisting and hopping. One of them was Woody and Flora Eaton, a big-boned widow out of luck who did the laundry and housework at the Bar JR. Many a dudine had tried to snare Woody for that first dance, but he always picked a native.

I said this is a sample, and I mustn't drag it out. In those four hours at the hall I heard much and saw much, but left around one-thirty no wiser.

I heard a girl in a cherry-colored shirt call across to Sam Peacock, one of the two wranglers at Farmham's, who came late, "Get a haircut, Sam, you look awful," and his reply, "I ain't so bad now. You should have seen me when I was a yearling, they had to tie my mother up before she'd let me suck."

I saw Johnny Vawter and Woody bounce a couple of boiled dudes who were trying to take the accordion away from the musician. The hooch that had inspired them had been brought by them, which was customary. At the bar in a corner the only items available were fizz-water, ice, paper cups, soft stuff, and aspirin.

I heard more beats and off-beats, and saw more steps and off-steps, than I had heard and seen at all the New York spots I was acquainted with.

I heard a middle-aged woman with ample apples yell at a man about the same age, "Like hell they're milk-fake!" and saw her slap him hard enough to bend him.

I heard a dude in a dinner jacket tell a woman in a dress nearly to her ankles, "A sheet-snapper is not a prostitute. It's a girl or a woman who makes beds." I heard Gil Haight say to another kid, "Of course she's not here. She's got a baby to look after." I saw about eight dozen people, all kinds and sizes, look the other way, or stop talking, or give me the fish-eye, when I came near.

So back at the cabin, in bed under two blankets for the cold of the night, there was nothing for my mind to work on and it turned me loose for sleep.

That's the sample, but before skipping to Wednesday evening I must report an incident that occurred at the cabin late Tuesday afternoon. I had just got back from somewhere and was with Lily on what we called the morning terrace, the other one being the creek terrace, when a car came up the lane—a Dodge Coronet hardtop I had seen before—with two men in the front seat, and Lily said, "There they are. I was just going to tell you, Dawson phoned they wanted to see me. He didn't say why."

The car was there, at the edge of the lodgepoles, and Luther Dawson and Thomas R. Jessup were getting out. Seeing those two, I was so impressed that I didn't remember my manners and leave my chair until they were nearly to us. The defense counsel and the county attorney coming together to see the owner of the ranch Harvey Greve ran had to mean that something had busted wide open, and when I did get up I had to control my face to keep it from beaming. Their faces were not beaming as they exchanged greetings with us and took the chairs I moved up for them, but of course the county attorney's wouldn't be if something had happened that was messing up a murder case for him. Lily said their throats were probably dry and dusty after their drive and asked what they would like to drink, but they declined with thanks.

"It may strike you as a little irregular, our coming together," Dawson said, "but Mr. Jessup wanted to ask you something and we agreed that it would be more in order for *me* to do the asking, in his presence."

Lily nodded. "Of course. Law and order."

Dawson looked at Jessup. They were both Montana-born-and-bred, but one looked it and the other didn't. Dawson, around sixty, in a striped blue-and-green shirt with rolled-up sleeves, no tie, and khaki pants, was big and brawny and leathery, while the county attorney, some twenty years younger, was slim and trim in a dark gray suit, white shirt, and maroon tie. Dawson looked at me, opened his mouth, shut it again, and looked at Lily. "Of course you're not my client," he said. "Mr. Greve is my client. But you paid my retainer and have said you will meet the costs of his defense. So I'll just ask you, have you consulted—er, approached—anyone else about the case?"

Lily's eyes widened a little. "Of course I have."

"Who?"

"Well . . . Archie Goodwin. Mrs. Harvey Greve. Melvin Fox. Woodrow Stepanian. Peter Ingalls. Emmett Lake. Mimi Deffand. Mort—"

"Excuse me for interrupting. My question should have been more specific. Have you consulted anyone other than local people? Anyone in Helena?"

If she had been any ordinary woman I would have horned in, but with Lily I didn't think it was necessary. It wasn't. "Really, Mr. Dawson," she said, "how old are you? How many hostile witnesses would you say you have cross-examined?"

He stared at her.

"I suppose," she said, "that lawyers have as much right to bad habits as other people, but other people don't have to like them." She turned to me. "What about it, Archie? Is it any of his business whom I have or haven't consulted?"

"No," I said, "but that's not the point. From what he said, the question is actually being asked by Jessup, through him. It certainly is none of Jessup's business, and they both have a hell of a nerve. I don't know about Montana, but in New York if a prosecuting attorney asked the person who was paying the defense counsel who she had consulted, the Bar Association would like to know about it. Since you asked my opinion, if I were you I would tell both of them to go climb a tree."

She looked at one and then the other, and said, "Go climb a tree."

Dawson said to me, "You have completely misrepresented the situation, Mr. Goodwin."

I eyed him. "Look, Mr. Dawson. I don't wonder that you fumbled it; as you said, it's a little irregular. If you hadn't been fussed you would probably have handled it fine. Obviously something has happened that made Jessup think someone has been persuaded to butt in on his case, and he suspects that Miss Rowan did the persuading, and he wants to know, and so do you. Also obviously the way to handle it would have been to tell her what has happened and ask her if she had a hand in it, and it wouldn't hurt to say please. If you don't want to do it that way I guess you'll have to look around for a tree."

Dawson looked at the county attorney. Jessup said, "It would have to be understood that it's strictly confidential."

Dawson nodded. Lily said, "If you mean we have to promise not to tell anybody, nothing doing. We wouldn't broadcast it just for fun, but no promises."

Dawson turned to Jessup and asked, "Well, Tom?"

Jessup said, "I'd like to confer," rose, and said to Lily, "Will you excuse us briefly, Miss Rowan?"

Lily nodded, and for the conference they walked over to the hardtop and behind it, and Lily asked me if I had a guess. I held up crossed fingers and said one would get her two that there was going to be some kind of a break, but as to what kind and how much, her guess was as good as mine. I no longer had to control my face to keep it from beaming.

The conference didn't take long. I wouldn't have been surprised if Dawson had come back alone just to say he was sorry we had been bothered, but in a few minutes they both came and took their chairs, and Dawson said, "The decision was Mr. Jessup's, not mine. I want to make it clear that I am here at all only because he thought it proper, and I agreed." He focused on Lily. "If you won't promise, Miss Rowan, you won't, and I merely want to say that I join him in hoping that you and Mr. Goodwin will regard what he tells you as a confidence. If I told you, it would be hearsay, so he will."

In the last five days I had tried three times to get to Thomas R. Jessup for a private talk, and got stiff-armed. I'm not complaining, just reporting. There's no law requiring a prosecuting attorney to talk it over with any and all friends of the defendant. It was Morley Haight, the sheriff, who had questioned me as a possible suspect or material witness. I had seen Jessup only from a distance and was appreciating the chance to size him up.

He gave Lily a politician's smile and said, "I'm sorry there was a misunderstanding, Miss Rowan. Mr. Goodwin said it wouldn't hurt to say please, and I do say please. Please consider this a confidential communication. I confidently leave that to your discretion. Mr. Goodwin said we should tell you what happened, and I'm going to. It won't take long. Early this morning I had a phone call from a state official in Helena—a high official. He asked me to come to his office at my earliest convenience and bring my files on the Harvey Greve case. I drove to Helena and was with him nearly three hours. He wanted a complete detailed report, and after I dictated it to his secretary he asked questions, many questions."

He turned on the politician's smile again, for Lily, then for me, and back to her. "Now that was extraordinary. As far as I know, unprecedented, for the attor—for that state official to urgently summon a county attorney to Helena to report in detail on a case he is preparing. And a *murder* case. Of course I asked him what had caused such sudden and urgent interest, but I got no satisfaction. When I left his office I had absolutely no idea of the reason for it; I couldn't even guess. I was twenty miles or more on my way back to Timberburg before it occurred to me that you might possibly have—er—intervened. You are concerned about Harvey Greve—properly, quite properly. You have retained Luther Dawson, an eminent member of the Montana bar, in his behalf. I know nothing of any political connections you may have, but a woman of your standing and wealth and background must be—must know many important people. So I turned around and drove back to Helena and went to see Mr. Dawson and described the situation to him. He said he knew nothing of any approach to the—to that official, and after some discussion he agreed that it would be reasonable to ask you about it, and he phoned you. I am not suggesting that you may have acted improperly, not at all. But if a high state official is going to—er—interfere with my handling of an important case, I have a right to know why, and naturally I want to know, and naturally Mr. Dawson does too, as counsel for the defense." The smile again. "Of course if what I have said was confidential, anything you say will be confidential too."

If they had known Lily as well as I did they would have known that the little circular movement of the toe of her shoe meant that she was good and sore. Also one of her eyes, the left, was slightly narrower than the other, which was even worse. "You're asking me," she said, "if I have pulled some strings with someone in Helena."

"Well . . . I wouldn't put it in those terms."

"I would and do. What I say isn't confidential, Mr. Jessup. *I* am suggesting that *you* have acted improperly. You're on the other side. Why should you ask me anything at all or expect me to tell you anything? If you'll go and sit in the car, Mr. Dawson will come in a minute."

"I assure you, Miss Rowan—"

"Damn it, do you want Mr. Goodwin to drag you?" She stood up, presumably to help me drag.

Jessup looked at me, then at Dawson. Dawson shook his head. Jessup, not smiling, got up and went, dignified, in no hurry. When he was in the car, some twenty paces away, Lily turned to the counsel for the defense. "I don't know if you've acted improperly or not, Mr. Dawson, and I don't care. Even if it was proper I don't like it, but I'll relieve your mind so you can use it for representing your clients, including Harvey Greve. I have approached or consulted no one 'other than local people,' no one in Helena or anywhere else, and I have no idea why a state official is interested in the case. Have you, Archie?"

"No."

"Then that's settled. Let's go get a drink." She headed for the cabin door, and I followed.

Inside, she went left, to the door to the long hall, but I stayed in the big room long enough to see Dawson join Jessup in the car and take the wheel. When the car had disappeared around a bend in the lane I proceeded to the hall and on to the kitchen. Lily was putting ice cubes in a pitcher, and Mimi was at the center table, slicing tomatoes brought by me from Vawter's.

"I'm trying to remember," Lily said, "if I was ever as mad as I am now."

"Oh, sure," I said. "More than once." I got out my wallet and produced two singles and offered them. "You win, damn it."

"Win what?"

Mimi's round blue eyes, which fitted her round face, which fitted all her other roundnesses, darted a glance at the bills and returned to the tomatoes. We talked as freely in her presence as Wolfe and I did in Fritz's. "I said," I told Lily, "that one would get you two that there was going to be some kind of a break. Here's the two. There will be no break."

"But I didn't take the bet. How do you know? If a high state official is interested—"

"Yeah, the Attorney General." I stuck the bills in a pocket and brought gin and vermouth from a shelf. "He almost said it once. Haven't you guessed who that report was for?"

"No." She cocked her head at me. "So you *have* approached somebody."

"No, not me. But one will get you ten that I know who did. I'm a detective, I figure things. I mailed that letter Saturday. He got it yesterday morning, and when he went up to the orchids he was harder for Theodore to take than usual. His appetite was off at lunch. Actually I am not absolutely essential to his convenience and comfort and welfare, nobody is, but he comes close to thinking I am. My letter left it wide open when he could expect me back—a week, a month, two months, no telling—and he hates uncertainty."

"So he phoned the Attorney General of Montana and demanded a complete detailed report pronto."

"No, but he phoned somebody." The ingredients were in and I started stirring. "There are a lot of people who are grateful for something he did, even after paying the bill, and a few of them are the kind who might phone a governor or even a president, let alone an attorney general. He phoned one of them, maybe more than one, and *he* phoned Helena. It wasn't any great favor to ask, just a report. The gist of it will probably be that the evidence against Harvey is all wool, from Montana sheep and two yards wide. If by phone he may have it already, and his appetite for dinner will be even worse." I looked at my wrist. "He's at the table now. It's seven-thirty-two in New York."

I put the glass rod down, picked up the pitcher, and poured. As she picked up her glass she said, "I admit that's good guessing, but you're not sure. Anyway I'm not. There *could* be a break." She raised the glass high. "To Harvey."

"One will get you ten. To Harvey."

If she had taken my ten-to-one offer, whether I had made a bad bet or not would have depended on whether what happened twenty-six hours later, around eight o'clock Wednesday evening, should be regarded as a break, and that would have depended on who did the regarding. I had spent the day scouting around making useless motions, trying to find a stone with something under it, and it was getting me down. At the supper table I had certainly contributed nothing to help to make it a jolly meal, and when the coffee was finished I had said I had a letter to write and gone to my room. I did want to write something, but not a letter. I was going to do something desperate, something I had never done before: write down every damned fact I had collected in ten days, at least every fact that could conceivably mean anything, and try to find connections or contradictions that would point somewhere. I was at the table by an open window, with a pad and a supply of pencils, considering where to start, when I heard a car coming up the lane. I couldn't see it because my room was on the creek side. The others were closer than I was, and the fact that I jumped up instantly and scooted to the big room showed what shape I was in. Pitiful. Diana was at the piano and Lily was at the screen door looking out, and I joined her. The car was there, a taxi from Timberburg. It would soon be dusk, but there was light enough to see the man at the wheel stick his head out of the window and call, "Is this Lily Rowan's place?"

I opened the door and stepped out and said yes, and the rear door of the taxi opened and a man climbed out, backwards. His big broad behind was Nero Wolfe's, and when he straightened up and turned around, so was his big broad front. Lily, at my elbow, said, "The mountain comes to Mohammed," and we crossed the terrace to meet him.

IV

WOLFE NEVER SHAKES HANDS with a woman, and rarely with a man, but out in God's country people loosen up more, and when his hand left mine he actually offered it to Lily as he said, "My apologies. I should have telephoned. You probably resent unexpected callers, as I do, but I dislike the telephone and I have used it too much these two days. I'll not disturb you. I had to see Mr. Goodwin."

"I make allowances," Lily said, "for callers who have come two thousand miles. Your luggage is in the car?"

"It is in Timberburg. Near there. At a place called Shafer Creek Motel." To me: "I have a suggestion. That man is foolhardy and his vehicle may collapse at any moment. If one is available here, I'll send him off and you can drive me back after we have conferred."

I turned to Lily. "As you know, he thinks all machinery acts on whim. If you won't need the car—"

"This is silly," she said. To Wolfe: "Of course you'll sleep here. There's a room with a bed. After a day in airplanes and cars, *you* must be about to collapse. Archie will tell the man to go and bring your luggage, and I'll show you your room. It has a bath. Have you had dinner?"

"Miss Rowan. I will not impose—"

"Now listen. You're used to having people at your mercy; now you're at mine. My car will not be available. Have you had dinner?"

"I have eaten, yes. There will be a bill to pay at that place."

I said I'd see to it and went and talked with the hackie. He didn't like the idea of another round trip, but agreed that that would be better than sticking there until his fare was ready to return when I said it might be long after midnight, and I gave him money for the motel bill. When he had turned around and rolled down the lane I entered the cabin by the door to the long hall, kept going, found the last door standing open, and entered. Wolfe was sitting in a chair by the open window with his chin down and his eyes closed. Lily had switched the light on. I stopped three paces in and looked at him. He was probably, at that moment, the only man in Monroe County wearing a vest, which of course was the same dark blue as the jacket and trousers. He had changed at the motel; the cuffs and collar of the yellow shirt were smooth and clean. The blue four-in-hand was a little darker than the suit, and so was the homburg there on the table. There was barely enough room for his hips between the arms of the wicker chair.

I asked, "Have a nice trip?"

He said, "There's a brook out there," and opened his eyes.

"Berry Creek. If we had known you were coming there could have been trout for breakfast. Are you staying long?"

"Pfui."

There were two other chairs in the room and I went to one of them and sat. "That's my mount's name. Miss Rowan named her mare Cat because she moves like one, and I named my horse, mine when I'm here, Pfui, because he's a little tricky. The natives pronounce it Fee. If you're going to do some mountain riding I recommend a palomino named Spotty, because with your bulk—"

"Shut up."

I didn't intend to, but I did, because Lily entered with a tray, and I got up to take it. On it were two glasses, a bottle of beer, an opener, a pitcher of milk, and paper napkins. "I saw to towels," she said. "I brought only one bottle of beer because I suppose he likes it cold. Do you need anything?"

"If we do I'll get it. We may need you, so don't wander off."

She said she wouldn't, and left. I put the tray on a table that Wolfe could reach, and he picked up the bottle, inspected the label—Mountain Brewery, Butte—took the opener and used it, and poured.

"It isn't bad," I said. "There's another brand that I think they put copper in."

He held the glass until the bead was down just right, took a sip, made a face, took a healthy swig, and licked foam from his lips. "I would prefer," he said, "to go to bed. I doubt if my brain will function properly, but I'll try. I received your letter."

"I suspected you had when I saw you get out of the car."

"It came Monday, day before yesterday. It didn't adequately describe the situation. I needed to know more about it, and I telephoned three men. The third one, Mr. Oliver McFarland—you remember him."

"Certainly."

"He was able and willing to oblige me. He has extensive banking and mining interests in this area. At his instigation I received, late yesterday afternoon, a telephone call from the Montana Attorney General. If the facts are as he reported them, you might as well return with me in the morning."

I nodded. "I expected this too when I saw you get out of the car. This is going to take a while, and there's a bigger and better chair in another room. If you'll vacate that one

I'll take it and make a trade. I'm as uncomfortable looking at you as you are in it."

He started to stand, but his hips caught between the arms and lifted the chair. He pushed it down and was free and up, and I took the chair and went, out, the length of the hall, and into the big room. Lily was there with Diana and Wade Worthy over by the fireplace, probably telling them that another guest had arrived. Seeing me, she said, "I should have suggested that. The one over there?"

It was the one I would have picked, over by the bookshelves. I moved it, put the one I had brought in its place, picked up the bigger one, which had a seat pad covered with what had once been the hide on a deer's belly, upturned it to put it on top of my head, and went back to the room. In that short time the beer bottle had been emptied, and after depositing the chair I went to the kitchen and brought another one; and I poured a glass of milk and went to my chair with it. Wolfe looked better, and of course felt better, in the roomier seat.

"I'll give you just the skeleton," I said, "and the flesh and skin can be added as required. If I'm more outspoken than usual it's probably because I'm on leave of absence without pay. First, I do not think you came to haul me back. You know me almost as well as I know you. I wrote you that one will get you fifty that Harvey's clean, and you know I don't give those odds unless I'm dead sure. I think you came to get *my* facts and then hurry it up by telling me what to do. I suppose you know, from the Attorney General, that Harvey's daughter had a baby this spring, and she told Harvey and Carol, his wife, that the father was Philip Brodell, a dude who was here last summer at a nearby ranch, and before long everybody knew it."

"Yes. Those are facts?"

"Sure. Then Brodell came again this summer, on Monday, July twenty-second. Three days later—"

"I interrupt. You're on leave without pay, but permit me. About three o'clock Thursday afternoon he went up a hill alone to pick berries. When he didn't return, even for the evening meal, there was concern, and when dark approached a search was begun. His favorite area for berries was known. Around nine-thirty his body was found by a man named Samuel Peacock on a boulder near the top of the hill. He had been shot twice, in the shoulder and in the neck. No bullets were found, but the wounds indicated a high-powered gun. The medical evidence was that he had died between three and six o'clock. The first limit was of course established, since he had been seen alive by four people around three o'clock; the second limit is probably correct. Do you challenge any of that?"

"No." I took a sip of milk. "That must have been quite a phone call. I hope he didn't call collect."

"He didn't. I asked many questions. You don't dispute the motive for Mr. Greve?"

"Of course not."

"Then to opportunity. He has no alibi for that afternoon from one o'clock on. He says he was on horseback looking for stray cattle, but he was alone. The horse could have taken him within about a mile of where the body was found. Challenge?"

"No."

"Then to means. Three guns of the kind indicated were available to him, two in his house and one in the sleeping quarters of men employed at the ranch. Challenge?"

"None you would buy, or a jury. His wife and daughter say the guns were there in the house, and Mel Fox says his was where it belonged, in his room. All right, they would, and Mel was out on a horse too."

"Then to particulars. The only other people with any discernible motive, the same motive as his, have alibis that have been checked and verified. I wasn't given their names, but—"

"Harvey's wife and daughter and a kid named Gilbert Haight. The wife and daughter, okay. The kid is on my list. His father is the county sheriff. He wanted to marry the daughter and says he still does—the kid, not the sheriff."

"Indeed." His brow was up. "You challenge his alibi?"

"I've worked some on it. The big trouble is I'm a dude. A dude out here is in about the same fix as a hippie in a Sunday school. Communication problems. You would see if you stayed, especially dressed like that, with that vest and hat. Any more particulars?"

"Yes. The day after Mr. Brodell arrived Mr. Greve said in the hearing of two men, 'A varmint with that thick a hide isn't fit to live.' Also—"

"He said ain't, not isn't. I heard him. You could stand the 'varmint,' but the 'ain't' was too much for you."

"The meaning was intact. Also, on Friday afternoon, the day after Brodell was killed, he drove to Timberburg and bought a bottle of champagne, which was unprecedented, and that evening he and his wife and daughter drank it. Also—"

"That *was* a phone call. Knowing how Harvey felt about Brodell, I was surprised he didn't buy two bottles, or a case and throw a party." I drank milk.

"And the next day, Saturday, when Brodell's father, who had come from St. Louis for the body, went to see Mr. Greve, he assaulted him."

"He clipped him and gave him a shiner. That was regrettable, no matter what the father had said to ask for it, since he's too old to be poked, but everybody knows that it's not a good idea to pull Harvey's nose or loosen his cinch. Also?"

"Isn't that enough?"

"It's probably enough for a jury, and that's the nut. That covers the phone call?"

"Sufficiently."

"Then it's my turn. In that letter I offered you fifty to one, and I still do. I know Harvey Greve and so does Miss Rowan. I haven't got one measly scrap of evidence for him, and none against anyone else, but I know him. Did the Attorney General mention that the first bullet that hit Brodell, in the shoulder, came from behind him?"

"No." He had opened the second bottle and poured.

"Well, it did. He was standing on a boulder, facing uphill, picking huckleberries, and X sneaked from downhill to easy range. The first bullet turned him around, so he was facing X when the second bullet got him in the neck and killed him. All right, that settles it. X was not Harvey Greve. I'll believe that Harvey Greve shot a man in the back, no warning, when I see you cut up a dill pickle, put maple syrup on it, and eat it with a spoon. And even if I could believe he shot a man in the back I still wouldn't believe he shot Brodell. Everybody knows there's no better shot around. If he shot at a man's back he wouldn't hit his shoulder. And the second shot, in the neck? Nuts."

He was frowning. He drank and put the glass down. "Archie. Your emotions are blocking your mental processes. If it is generally known that he is a good shot, making it appear that X wasn't would be a serviceable subterfuge."

"Not for Harvey. He hasn't got that kind of mind. Subterfuge is not only not in his vocabulary, it's not in his nature. But that's just talk. The point is that *he would not sneak up on a man and shoot him in the back*. Not a chance. Hell, make it a hundred to one."

The wrinkles of the frown were deeper. "This must be flummery. Certainly it isn't candor. Basing a firm conclusion of a man's guilt or innocence—not merely a conjecture—solely on your knowledge of his character? That's tommyrot and you know it. Pfui."

I gave him a wide grin. "Good. Now I've got you cold. You were right, your brain isn't functioning properly. Less than three years ago you formed a firm conclusion on Orrie Cather's guilt or innocence solely on Saul Panzer's knowledge of his character. You also consulted Fred and me, but we were on the fence. Saul decided it.* It's too bad I don't rate as high as Saul. And I have backing. Miss Rowan's conclusion is as firm as mine, but I admit she's a woman. There's a plane that leaves Helena at eleven in the morning. If I find I can't make it back in time to vote on November fifth I'll send for an absentee ballot."

The frown was gone, but his lips had tightened to a thin straight line. He poured the rest of the second bottle, watched the bead go down, picked up the glass, and drank. When his lips had been licked, they didn't tighten again. He twisted his head around for a look at the open window, put his hands on the chair arms to pry his seventh of a ton up, turned to the window, pulled it shut, sat down again, and asked, "Is there an electric blanket?"

"Probably. I'll ask Miss Rowan. When I went to bed at two o'clock Sunday morning it was thirty-six above. I'll make a concession. I'll drive you to Helena. To catch that plane we'll have to leave by seven o'clock, and I'd better phone if you want to be sure of a seat."

He took in air through his nose, all he had room for, say half a bushel, and let it out through his mouth. That wasn't enough, and he did it again. He looked at the bed, then at the

* *Death of a Doxy* (New York: The Viking Press, 1966).

dresser, then at the door to the bathroom, and then at me. "Who slept in this room last night?"

"Nobody. It's a spare."

"Bring Miss Rowan and— No, you're on leave. Will you please ask Miss Rowan if it will be convenient for her to join us?"

"Glad to." I went. As I passed the door of Wade's room the sound of his typewriter, not the Underwood, came through. In the big room Diana, with a magazine, and Lily, with a book, were on chairs near the fireplace, where six-foot logs were burning as usual of evenings. I told Lily her new guest wanted to know if it would be convenient for her to join us, and she put the book down and got up and came. On the way down the hall she asked no questions, which was like her and therefore no surprise. She knew from experience that if I knew something she should know, I had a tongue.

I was supposing that he was going to ask her something about Harvey's character, but he didn't. When she crossed to him and asked if she could do something he tilted his head back and said, "You'll oblige me if you sit. I don't like to talk up to people, or down. I prefer eyes at a level."

I moved the third chair up for her, and as she sat she spoke. "If I had known in advance you were coming I would have had a vase of orchids in the room."

He grunted. "I'm not in a humor for orchids. I'm in a predicament, Miss Rowan. I am indeed at your mercy. It is necessary for me to be in this immediate neighborhood, in easy touch with Mr. Goodwin, and I don't know how long. That place near Timberburg is not a sty, it's moderately clean, but it would be an ordeal, and it's at a distance. A self-invited guest is an abomination, but there is no alternative for me. May I occupy this room?"

"Of course." She was controlling a smile. "Archie has quoted you as saying once that a guest is a jewel on the cushion of hospitality. I know too much about you to expect you to be a jewel, but neither will you be an abomination. You could have just told Archie to come and tell me you were going to stay, instead of getting me in and asking me. You did it very nicely. I know how you feel about guests and hosts; I have dined at your house. Before you go to bed, tell me if you want anything."

"I presumed to ask Mr. Goodwin if there is an electric blanket."

"Certainly." She rose. "What else?"

"At the moment, nothing. Sit down—if you please. Mr. Goodwin is going to tell me what he has done and we're going to discuss what's to be done now. I'll ask questions, and you may know the answers to some of them better than he does. Will you remain?"

"Yes. I would like to."

"Very well. My first question deals with you. It must, if I am to be a guest in your house. How and where did you spend the afternoon of Thursday, July twenty-fifth?"

I don't want to give the impression that I am trying to sell the idea that Lily Rowan, in all respects and circumstances and 365 days in the year, is a perfect female biped. Anyone who tried to sell *me* that idea would have an argument. But there aren't many women who wouldn't have wasted time and words, one way or another, in reacting to that question, and she didn't react at all, she merely answered it.

"Most of it fishing," she said, "in the Fishtail River. In midsummer trout are scarce in the creek and to fill a creel you have to go to the river. Around one o'clock that day Archie and I were sitting at the edge of Cutthroat Pool eating a picnic lunch. We had left our horses at the end of the trail." She turned to me. "How far were we from Blue Grouse Ridge?"

"Oh, ten or twelve miles."

Back to Wolfe. "Blue Grouse Ridge is where Philip Brodell was killed. After lunch we caught fish and took a dip in
the river, which a polar bear would love, and watched bea-
vers repairing a dam in a creek, and Archie threw a rock at
a bear—black, not polar—who jumped into a pool to swim
across when he had a cutthroat on. It was nearly dark when
we got home, and Diana—she's a guest—said that Bill Farnham had phoned to ask if Philip Brodell was here."

"What's a cutthroat?"

"A trout with a red mark under the jaw. If I had a cap,
that would be a feather in it, using a word you didn't know."

"There are thousands of words I don't know." He turned
to me. "I concede that you may reasonably object that that
was unnecessary. If you had not conclusively eliminated
Miss Rowan, you would not have remained as her guest. I've
had a long hard day and I'm tired, and my wits are slow. I
haven't even asked you if *you* shot that man. Did you?"

"No. I was wondering why you didn't ask."

"I'm tired. But go ahead. If I find I can't keep up with
you I'll say so. Report."

"I'll have to know what for," I said. "You said you don't
know how long you'll stay. If you intend just to check our
conclusion on Harvey and wish us luck, there's no point
in—"

"How can I check your conclusion? I can only accept it
or reject it. Very well, I accept it. The length of my stay
depends on how long it will take us to establish his innocence."

" 'Us'?"

"Yes."

I raised a brow. "I don't know. You mean well and I
deeply appreciate it, but there are a couple of snags. One,
we have never worked together like this. We're equals,
fellow guests of Miss Rowan. You wouldn't be paying me to

run errands and follow instructions and bring anybody you wanted to see, and I would be free to balk if I thought—"

"Nonsense. I'm reasonable and so are you."

"Not always, especially you. I have known you to assume —but there's no use in going into that now. It *might* work. We can give it a try. Second, you'd be in the same fix as me, only worse. Nobody would tell you anything. I've been here before, as you know, but men who have pitched horseshoes and played pinochle and chased coyotes with me, and women who have danced with me, clam up when I want to discuss murder. I've had ten days of that, and you're not only a dude, you're a complete stranger and a freak that wears a vest. Even if you asked me to go and bring A or B or C, and I brought him, you would know as much when he left as when he came. He might tell you how old he is. I doubt if—"

"Archie. If your conclusion about Mr. Greve is sound, and I have accepted it, someone knows something that will demonstrate it. Will my presence make it harder for you?"

"No."

"Very well. Miss Rowan has said I may occupy this room. I would appreciate a full report."

"It would take all night. We'd better go to bed and—"

"I can't go to bed until my luggage comes."

"Okay. More beer?"

He said no. I shifted in my chair and crossed my legs. "This will be the longest row of goose eggs I have ever reported. I have spent ten days on it, and as I said, I haven't got a scrap of evidence pointing to anyone. There are plenty of possibles. Two of them are your fellow guests, very handy for grilling: Miss Diana Kadany, a New York actress so far off Broadway but hoping to make it on, and Mr. Wade Worthy, a writer, working on the outline of a book he's going to produce about Miss Rowan's father. They both qualify on means. In a cupboard in the storeroom, which is down the hall, there's a gun that would have done fine—a Mawdsley Special double-decker. Either of them would have trouble hitting a barn with it, let alone a barn door, as they proved a couple of weeks ago when Diana and I took on Worthy and Miss Rowan for a target tournament, but that fits in, since X was a lousy shot. So there's two possibles, right here. Morley Haight, the sheriff, didn't check the gun, with Miss Rowan's permission, until Friday afternoon. It was clean, but there had been plenty of time to see to that."

"His motive? Or hers?"

"I'll come to it. On opportunity they also qualify. Mimi Deffand, who will cook your breakfast unless you would rather do it yourself, had the day off, with Miss Rowan and me picnicking at the river, and she spent it in Timberburg. I haven't pumped my fellow guests, but it appears from conversation that Diana picnicked too, up the creek at what we call the second pool, and got back around six o'clock, so Worthy was here alone. Beautiful. No alibi for either of them, and they would be hot if there was the slightest smell of motive. Neither of them had ever seen Brodell, they say. I saw him a few times last year—he and Farnham came for supper once, and we went there—and he liked shows and had been to New York, I don't know how often. I thought of writing Saul to ask him to see if he could dig up a contact between Brodell and either of them, but you know what a job that is—at five Cs a week, which is what it would cost Miss Rowan."

"That wouldn't break me," Lily said, "but I simply can't believe they were lying when they said they had never seen him or heard of him. That was the day after he came, when I told them the father of Alma's baby was back."

"I missed a chance," I said, "of seeing them with him, but I didn't know he would be dead in about twenty hours.

Farnham invited Miss Rowan and her guests to supper Wednesday, and she and Diana went, but Worthy and I didn't. I have no ironbound rule against eating a meal with a man who has seduced a girl, but Brodell wasn't on my list of pets anyhow, so I skipped it and won eighty cents at gin rummy with Worthy, who was off his feed and wanted to go to bed early."

I flipped a hand. "They're good samples of the possibles. At the Farnham place there are a cook and houseworker, two wranglers, four dudes, and Farnham himself. At the Bar JR there are Flora Eaton, who does laundry and house chores, Mel Fox, in charge now with Harvey gone, and two cowboys. Carol and Alma, the wife and daughter, are crossed off—not just their mutual alibi, I'll tell you why when we're on details. That's fifteen possibles who were within walking distance, and add the adult population of Monroe County. Anyone could have driven here, and about two miles beyond where you turned off on the lane to this cabin he could have left the car and climbed the ridge. Farnham says that last year Brodell was in Timberburg three or four times, and I spent three days there digging up contacts."

"He took a box of huckleberries to the girl who sells tickets at the movie theater," Lily said.

Wolfe grunted. "Was it a mania? Did he come here from St. Louis only to pick huckleberries?"

I said no, he also rode horses and fished. "Much of my three days in Timberburg was spent on Gilbert Haight—on people who know him. Besides the Greves, he's the only one with any visible known motive. His alibi could be a phony, but to crack it you'd have to prove that at least three people are liars, and you couldn't expect any help from the county men, since his father is the sheriff. One of the aspects of the situation is Sheriff Haight's personal slants on it. It suits him fine to have Harvey on the hook for murder, because

Harvey was pretty active against him when he ran for sheriff. The county attorney, Thomas R. Jessup, is not so keen on it because Harvey helped some to get *him* elected, but he can't stall even if he wants to because he's stuck with the evidence Haight has collected. Haight would love it if Jessup got a black eye, and vice versa, and it would be nice to find a way to take advantage of that, but I haven't come up with one. I can't even get to Jessup, probably because he thinks the case against Harvey is so strong that he has to go along."

Wolfe nodded. "The Attorney General told me that the county attorney is a man of ability and integrity and good judgment."

"Which may be true, in spite of something he did yesterday. He came here yesterday afternoon with the defense counsel, the lawyer Miss Rowan has hired, to ask her some questions. He wanted to know—*they* wanted to know—if Miss Rowan had—"

I stopped because I heard a car out front. Lily rose, but I said I would go, and when I did she came along, down the hall and on out to the terrace. It was the taxi, and the hackie had opened the rear door and was lifting out a big tan leather suitcase which hadn't been out of the basement storeroom in the brownstone on West 35th Street for six years. The new guest's luggage had come.

V

AT A QUARTER PAST THREE the next afternoon, Thursday, Nero Wolfe and I were sitting on rocks, facing each other. We had been there more than three hours. The top of his rock, about chair-height from the ground, was level and flat and fairly smooth, and had plenty of room for his rump. Mine was more rugged, level enough but far from smooth, but I had eased it by standing from time to time. To Wolfe's right there was a tangle of brush, to his rear and left there were trees, mostly jack pine, and to his front, at a distance of some ten yards, Berry Creek was skimming and skittering over its rocky bottom toward the cabin, which was about half a mile away.

The night before, after leaving him in his room, Lily and I had agreed that he shouldn't be pampered. He was in rough country and would have to rough it. If he wanted any of the frills to which he was accustomed, such as breakfast on a tray in his room, he would load it in the kitchen and carry it in himself. He would make his bed or not make it, as he chose, as we all did. I had gone back to his room, found him already under the electric blanket, and told him the household routine, and he had grunted and turned over.

The breakfast hour was nine o'clock, and usually we all made it unless there was something special on the program—except Diana, who often slept late. That morning she was right on time, probably because there was a new man to practice on. Of course Mimi knew Wolfe's reputation on food, and I gave her a grin when I saw her putting paprika on the scrambled eggs, and again when I saw that she had nearly doubled the amount of bacon and bread slices for toast. Also instead of three kinds of jam on the table there were six. As Wade Worthy sat he said, "A reputation like yours has advantages, Mr. Wolfe. Such abundance!"

"Don't mind him," Diana said. She patted Wolfe's sleeve with two fingertips. "He's just jealous. I would love to butter a toast for you."

Wolfe declined the offer but didn't scowl at her. A guest is a jewel. Mimi brought another platter of eggs, and they had paprika too.

After breakfast Wolfe and I had gone to his room and I helped him unpack. I admit that smacked of pampering, but I was curious. And as I had suspected when I had helped the hackie with the luggage, he had prepared for an extended stay when he left home; there was another suit—the brown worsted with little green specks—another pair of shoes, five shirts, ten pairs of socks, and so forth, including four books, one of which he may have brought along for possible reference. It was *Man's Rise to Civilization as Shown by the Indians of North America from Primeval Times to the Coming of the Industrial State*. By Peter Farb. He may have supposed that a Blackfoot or Chippewa might be a suspect and he wanted to know how their minds work.

When everything was unpacked and in place in drawers and the closet, I had made a suggestion. "If it's to be a full report, it will take hours, and you're used to a larger room. Mine is twice the size of this, or there's the big room, or the terrace. You would probably—"

"No," he said.

"No? No report?"

"Not here. Last evening I was constantly aware that we might be overheard, outside through the window or inside through the door or wall. Our discussions of problems have always been in a soundproofed room, secure, no unwanted interruptions. Whereas here—there are three women on the premises, and one of them is a congenital pest. Confound it, can't we go somewhere?"

"If you mean somewhere under a roof, no. Outdoors, almost anywhere. I know dozens of nice spots for a picnic. The storeroom shelves aren't as full as they were a month ago, but there's sturgeon, ham, dried beef, four kinds of cheese—we can take our pick. There's half a roast turkey in the kitchen refrigerator. The temperature of the creek is perfect for beer."

"How far?"

"Anywhere from a hundred yards to a hundred miles. If we take horses . . ."

He glared at me and asked where the storeroom was.

It was nearly eleven o'clock when we hit the trail because he spent a good twenty minutes looking over the storeroom shelves and cupboards, and anyway I had to go and tell Lily and change my shoes and pack the knapsack with the grub. When we left, by the morning terrace, Diana, there in a chair, looked up at Wolfe and put on a pout and said she would have loved to come along, and he didn't actually growl at her.

So at a quarter past three there we were, on the rocks, with the lunch remains, including three empty beer cans, back in the knapsack, and the report delivered and questions answered. Of course the report had not been full, if "full" means nothing left out, but he had the picture, including names and connections and guesses that had fizzled—a thousand details that I haven't put in *this* report. The trunks of three saplings were rubbing against the edge of his rock, and he had tried twenty times to use them for a back rest, but it made his feet leave the ground and dangle, so it was no go. Now he tried it again, said, "Grrrrh," gave up, slid forward on the rock, stood up, and started to speak but didn't because something behind me caught his eye. He raised an arm to aim a finger and asked, "What's that?"

I twisted around. A big gray bird had landed on a branch only twenty feet away and only six feet up. "Fool hen," I said. "A kind of grouse that thinks everybody goes by its favorite saying, Peace on earth, good will to grouse. If I went slow and smooth, peaceful, I could walk over and pick it off."

"Are they palatable?"

"Sure. Very tasty."

"Then why are there any left?"

"I've asked about that, and apparently the feeling is that if a wild critter hasn't got sense enough to act wild, to hell with it. So they call it fool hen. But you don't see many of them."

He moved, and with his hand on a tree for balance shook his right leg and then his left, to get his pants legs down. "I'm going to try something," he said. "A telephone call. You wrote that Miss Rowan's line might be tapped. If so, by whom? The sheriff, or the county attorney?"

"The sheriff."

"Then I can't use it for this call. Is there one I can use with assurance?"

I nodded. "At Lame Horse. A New York call? Saul?"

"No. Mr. Veale."

"I haven't mentioned anyone named Veale."

"I have—not by name, by title. The Attorney General in Helena. I have his number. He knows I'm here. Mr. Mc-Farland telephoned him again yesterday, at my request, to tell him I was coming, and I went to see him when I got to Helena. I need to ask him something."

I was up, getting the knapsack strapped on. I said the car would probably be available, but if not I could borrow one at the ranch, and we moved. Since we were equals I could have demanded to know what he wanted to ask the Attorney General, but it didn't matter because nothing he asked anybody could have made the situation any worse.

Going back was tougher for him than coming had been, because it was downhill and there were a couple of places where anyone might do a tumble, but he made it without a scratch. The car was there, and I went in the cabin, got rid of the knapsack, went to Wolfe's room to get a phone number from a slip of paper in a drawer, found Lily on the creek terrace, told her we had an errand in Lame Horse, and asked if the car was free. She said yes and asked if we would be back in time for supper, and I said yes, we were just going to make a phone call which I would tell her about later. Outside, Wolfe had taken the car for granted and got in, which was a little cheeky for a guest, and he was in the front, which was unusual. In his Heron sedan, which I drive, he always sits in the back, where there is a strap for him to grab when the car decides to try climbing a curb or jostling some other car it doesn't like. I got in behind the wheel and we rolled. As we turned onto the road at the end of the lane a wild animal scooted out from a tuft and bounded hell-bent for the brush, and he asked, "Native hare?"

"That depends," I said, "on whether a jackrabbit is a hare. I've never looked it up, but I will. They are *not* palatable." I circled around a rock patch. "The man we're going to ask to let us use his phone is Woodrow Stepanian. As I reported, he's one of the few people who thinks Harvey is clean."

"The Hall of Culture. You told me three years ago that he tried to get you to read Bacon's essays."

"I see you brought your memory along. It may come in handy." I slowed the car to ease down the bank of a gully and climb back up. "He will expect you to shake hands.

Everybody you meet out here will, and you've got enough built-in points against you without adding another one."

"I resent any formality requiring bodily contact."

"Yeah, I know. But what's one more hardship after all you've gone through since yesterday morning?"

He compressed his lips and turned his head to watch gophers diving into holes.

At four in the afternoon on a weekday, in one respect Lame Horse is a big improvement on New York—the parking problem. Except Saturday nights, there isn't any. When we got out, right at the entrance of the Hall of Culture, Wolfe stood there a minute, swiveling his head for a survey of the surroundings before preceding me inside. We crossed to a table by the wall where a four-sided game of Scrabble was in progress, though only one man was there—Woody—with the names of the four players written on cards by the racks: William Shakespeare, John Milton, Ralph Waldo Emerson, and Woodrow Stepanian. I had seen that performance before, with different players, except Woody of course. He rose as we approached, and I pronounced names, and Wolfe took the offered hand like a gentleman. I concede that when he does shake he does it right.

"It is an honor," Woody said. "I bow to you. Do you play Scrabble?"

Wolfe shook his head. "I don't play games. I like using words, not playing with them."

"We came to ask a favor," I said. "We have to make a private phone call and it could be that the sheriff has a tap on Miss Rowan's line. She sends her regards. May we use your phone?"

He said yes, certainly, looked down at the Scrabble game, muttered to himself, "Milton's turn," and went to the screen door and on out. Wolfe crossed to the desk in the corner where the phone was, and sat on a chair that was fine for

Woody but not for him, and I told him to dial the operator and give her the number. He made a face, as always when he had to use the phone, and lifted the receiver.

Since there was no extension for me I can report only one end of the talk. After he told somebody his name and asked for Mr. Veale, and a two-minute wait: "Yes, speaking. . . . No, I'm not in Timberburg, I'm staying at the cabin of Mr. Greve's employer, the woman who owns the ranch. . . . Yes, Miss Lily Rowan. I have decided that I should communicate with Mr. Jessup forthwith, and I need to know if you reached him. . . . Yes, I know, I understand the need for discretion. . . . No, he hasn't, but he doesn't know where I am. . . . Yes indeed, and I am obliged to you, and Mr. McFarland will be too."

He hung up and turned to me and said, "Get Mr. Jessup," frowned, and added, "if you please." Being my equal was an awful bother.

Having rung the office of the county attorney in Timberburg four times to try to get an appointment, I didn't have to look up the number. Standing at the end of the desk, I reached for the phone and dialed and told the female who answered that Nero Wolfe wanted to speak with Mr. Jessup, and in a minute his voice came.

"Mr. Wolfe?"

"Archie Goodwin. Here's Mr. Wolfe."

Again I can give only one end: "Mr. Jessup? Nero Wolfe. I believe Mr. Veale has spoken to you of me. . . . Yes, so he told me. I wish to talk with you, probably at some length, and not, I think, on the telephone. . . . Yes. . . . Certainly. . . . I would much prefer today. . . . Yes, I understand that. . . . No, I'm at a telephone in Lame Horse, in the office of Mr. Woodrow Stepanian. . . . No. I don't. You had better speak with Mr. Goodwin."

He held it out and I took it. "Archie Goodwin."

"Do you know where Whedon's Graveyard is?"

"Sure."

"I'll leave in about ten minutes—perhaps twenty—and meet you there. Will anyone be with you besides Mr. Wolfe?"

I said no, and he said all right and hung up. I told Wolfe, "We're to meet him at Whedon's Graveyard, which is a little farther from Timberburg than from here. About ten miles."

"A cemetery?"

"No. A long time ago a man named Whedon got the idea that he could grow wheat there and he tried it, and the story is that he starved to death, but I doubt that. This begins to look interesting. Jessup doesn't want you to come to his office because the sheriff's office is also in the courthouse." I looked at my watch: 4:55. "I'll ring Miss Rowan and tell her we'll be late for supper."

While I was doing that, and getting the charges from the operator, he took a look at a few items of cultural material. When we went out I expected to see Woody there, but he wasn't. He was with a little group in front of Vawter's, watching a race up the road a little—or rather, a chase—coming this way. A scrawny little guy in Levi's, no shirt, was loping down the middle of the road, and after him, some ten yards back, was a fat red-faced woman with a long leather strap. As he neared Vawter's the man yelled at the group, "Rope her! Goddammit, rope her!" He yelled it again when he saw Wolfe and me. When he was about even with us he swerved to the right, stumbled and nearly fell, and headed for a path which curved around the side of a house, with the woman nearly at his tail. She almost had him as they disappeared back of the house.

Wolfe looked at me with his brows up.

"Local routine," I said. "About once a month. Mr. and Mrs. Nev Barnes. She bakes bread and pies and sells them, and he snitches some of the proceeds and buys hooch from

a bootlegger named Henrietta. There's a theory that the
reason she doesn't hide the jack where he couldn't find it is
that it would gum the act. If he wasn't lit she would never
catch him. The reason he yells 'Rope her' is that one time a
couple of years ago a cowboy was over by the hitching-rack
trying a new rope he had just bought at Vawter's, and when
Nev saw him he yelled at him to rope her, and the cowboy
did, and ever since Nev always yells it."

"Was that her bread at breakfast?"

"Yes. Salt-rising. You ate four slices."

"It's quite edible." He went to the car and climbed in.
Woody came and I thanked him and paid for the calls,
waved to the Vawters, who were still out front, of course
wondering who that was with me, got in behind the wheel and
started the engine, and eased the car over the rough spot onto
the start of the blacktop.

We had gone three or four miles when Wolfe said, "You're
hitting bumps deliberately."

"I am not. It's the road. Try driving it *without* hitting
bumps. Also this is not your Heron with its special springs."
Bump. "Would it hurt to discuss what you're going to say to
Jessup?"

"Yes. Jouncing along like this? I'll decide what to say,
and how to say it, after I see him."

If you want to visit Whedon's Graveyard you have to
know exactly where it is. There's no sign and no lane to turn
into, though there probably was one when Whedon was on
his wheat caper. Now, just beyond a certain patch of aspen
at the edge of the blacktop, and just before a culvert over
a cut, you leave the road and turn right onto dry grass—dry
in August—circle around the foot of a slope, follow the rim
of a gulch for a couple of hundred yards, and there it is.
There is no visible reason for you to be glad you came. What
was presumably once a house with a roof is now a pile of

jackstraws for Paul Bunyan to play with if he happens by—
old logs and boards sticking up and out at crazy angles, and
others scattered around. Also, if you enjoy looking at bare
white bones, well weathered, there are some here and there,
where visitors have probably tossed them after taking a
look. Johnny Vawter says some of them are Whedon's, but
he admits he isn't a bone expert, and I have never checked
his claim that an undertaker in Timberburg agrees with him.

I had seen Jessup's car, a dark blue Ford sedan, and it
wasn't there. Except what I have described, nothing and
nobody was there. I turned the car around to head back,
killed the engine, and said, "A suggestion. If he's in the back
seat you'll have to twist around to face him. If you move to
the back and he gets in with me he'll have to do the twisting."

"I have never," he said, "had an important conversation
sitting in an automobile."

"Certainly you have. Once with Miss Rowan, once with
me, and a couple of others. Your memory's doing fine. You
said once that a signal function of the memory is discarding
what we want to forget. And where else would you like to
sit? This graveyard has no tombstones."

He opened the door, slid out backwards, opened the rear
door, and climbed in. I skewed around to face him and said,
"Much better. Some day you'll realize what a help I am."

"Pfui. Why am I here, two thousand miles from my
house?"

"To see justice done. To right a wrong. Now about Jessup.
For sizing him up it may help to know that he was born in
Montana, is forty-one years old, and is happily married with
three children. University of Montana, which is at Missoula.
In my report I didn't mention that Luther Dawson says Jessup would rather be a judge than a governor, he was fourth
in his class at law school, and he—and here he comes."

Since we were headed out we didn't have to twist our

necks to see the Ford leave the slope and bounce along the gulch rim. Twenty yards off it stopped, then came on again and nosed in alongside. I had thought it likely that he would have someone with him, not to be outnumbered, but he was alone. He got out, nodded to me, came to the rear door, said to Wolfe, "I'm Tom Jessup," and offered a hand through the open window. For a second I thought Wolfe was going to revert to normal on me, but he said, "I'm Nero Wolfe," and put out a hand to permit bodily contact. Jessup said he guessed our car was roomier than his, and we agreed, and he went around to the other side. I leaned across to open the front door, and he took the hint and got in.

He turned to me. "I came to see what Mr. Wolfe has to say, but first I'd like to just mention a point. You said the other day that you didn't know why a state official was interested in the case, and now it's evident that—well, that wasn't true. You did know."

"Now listen," I said. "Instead of calling me a liar, why not ask me? I didn't know that Mr. Wolfe had made a move until I saw him get out of a taxi yesterday evening. As evidence that *that* isn't a lie, if I had known he was coming I would have gone to Timberburg to get him, or even to Helena. Not that it matters now, since you're assuming that it was for him that the Attorney General wanted that report."

"Not assuming. I know it was." He slued around, putting a knee on the seat, to face the rear. "Mr. Wolfe, I'm an officer of the law. I have been told by a superior officer of the law that you have come to invest—er, to inquire into the Harvey Greve case, and he requested me—I'll call it 'requested'—to extend to you every possible courtesy. I try to—"

"Didn't he say 'cooperate'?"

"He may have. I try to show courtesy, in my official capacity as well as personally, to any and all of my fellow citizens, but my primary obligation is to the people of this county who chose me to serve them. I'll be frank with you. This is the first time I have received such a request from the Attorney General. I don't want to refuse it or ignore it unless I have to. I ask *you* to be frank with me. I want you to tell me what kind of pressure you brought to bear on Mr. Veale to persuade him to take that action."

Wolfe nodded. "Naturally you would like to know, and there are many officers of the law who wouldn't have bothered to ask. Did Mr. Veale mention any names?"

"Only yours—and Mr. Goodwin's."

"Then I can't fully match your frankness. 'Pressure' is probably too strong a word. I have no connections in Montana—political or professional or personal—none whatever; but a man I know in New York has. A man who is well disposed to me. Since Mr. Veale didn't name him, I can't, but I know him to be a man of probity and punctilio. I assume he merely asked a favor of Mr. Veale. I am sure he would bring no pressure to bear that you would consider shabby or corrupt—but of course that leaves open the question of the worth of my assurance. Of me. You don't know me."

"I knew your name. Most people do, even out here. I phoned two men in New York, one a district attorney, and was told, in effect, that your word is good but that anyone dealing with you should be sure he knows what your word is."

A corner of Wolfe's mouth raised a little—with him, a smile. "That could have been said of the Delphian oracle. Tell me how you would like my assurance phrased."

"You won't give me his name? Off the record?"

"It would be on *my* record. If Mr. Veale didn't, I can't." Wolfe cocked his head. "A question, Mr. Jessup. Why don't you ask what kind of cooperation I expect? It's conceivable

that you would have granted it even without a request from
Mr. Veale."

"All right, tell me what you expect."

Wolfe closed his eyes and in a moment opened them.
"I expect to be enabled to make an inquiry without intol-
erable hindrance. Mr. Goodwin has been trying to for ten
days and has been completely frustrated. He has had neither
a fulcrum or a lever. No one will tell him anything. He has
had no standing—not only no official standing, not even the
standing of an empowered agent of Mr. Greve, because the
attorney who has been hired by Miss Rowan believes that
Mr. Greve killed that man, as you do."

"It isn't merely a belief. It's a conclusion based on evidence."

"Evidence secured by Mr. Haight. I charge Mr. Haight
with nonfeasance amounting to malfeasance. He has an animus for Mr. Greve. Having gathered, as he thinks, enough
evidence against Mr. Greve to make a case, he has made no
effort whatever to explore other possibilities. There were
fifteen other people within walking distance of that spot that
Thursday afternoon, all of whom had had previous contact
with Mr. Brodell, and Mr. Haight has virtually ignored
them. I am not—"

"Can you support that?"

"I can," I said. "They won't open up about Brodell or
murder, but they will about Haight. Ask them."

"I am not including Mr. Greve's wife and daughter,"
Wolfe said, "because Mr. Goodwin and I have eliminated
them on evidence that convinces us, though it wouldn't convince you. Nor would you accept as decisive the evidence
that has persuaded us that Mr. Greve is innocent, but that
doesn't matter because what we want, all we want, is an
opportunity to inquire effectively. It's conceivable that no

evidence exists that will clear Mr. Greve, but we assert our right to try to find some. In order to—"

"I don't challenge that right. No one does. Go ahead."

"Pfui. That's twaddle and you know it. You might as well tell a man with no legs that you don't challenge his right to walk. What I ask, what Mr. Goodwin and I expect, is active support of that right. We can't get it from Mr. Haight, as you know, but we hope to get it from you. I have been told that in Montana a county attorney proceeds mostly on information supplied by the sheriff and the state police, but that he frequently investigates independently—himself, or members of his staff, or if necessary special investigators chosen by him. Mr. Goodwin and I want to investigate the Greve case for you. We want credentials. We are professionally qualified. We would not expect or accept any pay or reimbursement for expenses."

"I see." Jessup looked at me, saw only an open and manly phiz, ready to help, and went back to Wolfe. "That's it, huh? Mr. Veale suggested it?"

"No, I did. Presumably he thought it reasonable, or he wouldn't have asked you to see me. The purpose is obvious. Accredited by you, we would not be mere bumptious interlopers from outside—far outside. We would be seen and heard, and we could insist on answers to questions."

Jessup smiled, decided it rated better than that, and laughed—a hearty open-mouth laugh that would have been objectionable if it had been aimed at us, but it wasn't. If I had been sure it was for Sheriff Haight I would have joined in, but that was only a guess.

He eyed Wolfe. "This needs consideration."

Wolfe nodded. "And deserves it."

"I don't know if you realize the potential impact on me, on my—career. Any resentment you caused would be for you only temporarily, for me permanently. I would be—"

"Also any plaudits we earned would be for you permanently."

"Yes, if you earned any. I would be risking my future on your—uh—conduct. Obviously you hope to clear Greve, and on the evidence in hand you can't possibly prove that he's innocent unless you prove that someone else is guilty. Who?"

"I have no idea, and neither has Mr. Goodwin. We haven't even a specific suspicion. We have only our firm conclusion, on grounds that satisfy us but wouldn't satisfy you, that Mr. Greve is innocent, and we intend to demonstrate it."

"Even if I don't 'cooperate'?"

"Yes. If you won't give us a footing I think Mr. Veale might, but if not, we'll still have two advantages: Miss Rowan's financial resources and our competence as investigators. It might take months, even years, but we're committed by our resolution and self-esteem."

"Did Mr. Veale tell you that he would cooperate if I didn't?"

"No. He said he could, but not that he would."

"Then *you* threaten me."

"Mr. Jessup. You can't condemn an intention just by calling it a threat."

"No, but some intentions *are* threats. I was advised to make sure I know what your word is. You said, I quote, 'We haven't even a specific suspicion.' *I'll* specify. Do you suspect Gilbert Haight?"

"Only generally, along with others. He had a motive, but he has an alibi, apparently sound. Mr. Goodwin's attempts to test it have been futile, like all his other attempts. You said you would be risking your future on our conduct; you're risking it now on the conduct of Mr. Haight. What if you proceed on the evidence he has supplied, and try Mr. Greve and convict him, and a month later, or a year later, we produce evidence that establishes his innocence?"

Jessup straightened around in the seat, facing front, stretched his legs as far as there was room for, and stared at the dash. I have a theory about that kind of stare in such a situation: the fewer the blinks, the harder the thinking. If it's as little as three or four blinks a minute he's thinking as hard as his brain can manage, and Jessup blinked only eleven times in three minutes. Then they began to come faster, and he was back to normal when he turned around again to face Wolfe.

"I'll tell you something," he said. "You said I might have cooperated even without a request from Mr. Veale. I concur. I might have. By God, I think I would. But your coming at me through him gives it a slant I don't like, and I want to consider it. I want to confer on it with someone, and I'll let you know."

Wolfe was frowning. "Not, I trust, with Mr. Haight."

"Of course not. With the one person whose interests are always identical with mine. My wife. You'll hear from me soon."

"The sooner the better."

Jessup nodded. "Probably this evening. Where can I reach you? At Miss Rowan's?"

Wolfe, still frowning, said yes, and Jessup opened the door and got out, went to his car, and got in. When he backed at an angle to turn around, a log stopped him and he had to maneuver. That's why I always park facing out; I like a clean quick exit, aside from the fact that sometimes the situation demands it. As the Ford went jolting along the gulch rim I said, "So now it depends on a woman."

"He's an ass," Wolfe growled. "There are no two people alive whose interests are always identical."

"Yeah, a lawyer should know better. Also he's a damn liar. Without the Veale slant he wouldn't even have given you a nod, let alone come to Whedon's Graveyard to meet you." I turned the key and the engine took, and we moved. In three minutes it would be six o'clock, so I was glad I had phoned Lily. As we reached the blacktop I asked him whether he would rather go slow for the bumps, which would prolong it, or take them as they came and get it over with, but got no reply but a glare.

When we were about a mile from Lame Horse he suddenly spoke. "Stop the car."

His voice was louder than necessary, close to a shout, but it always was in a moving vehicle. Also no "please," but it was no time or place for etiquette. I slowed, eased off of the blacktop, set the brake, and said, "Yes?"

"Will Mr. Stepanian's telephone be available at this hour?"

"Probably. He has living quarters in the back."

"If it is, get Saul. What time is it in New York?"

"Eight o'clock. A little after. He'll be at home. Thursday's poker night."

"Get him. I don't like the possibility, however remote, that we are at table three times a day with a murderer, and for this we don't need credentials. Tell him we want to know if there was any contact between Miss Kadany or Mr. Worthy and Mr. Brodell during his visits to New York. Can you get pictures to send him—covertly?"

"Possibly, but I doubt if I need to. She's an actress, and he'll have no trouble getting pictures of her. For Worthy, his publisher will almost certainly have some. Perhaps I should ring Miss Rowan first and tell her."

"You'll tell her later, or I will. I'll pay Saul's fee and expenses."

"She will want to."

"Then she may. That's of no consequence."

I said okay and released the brake. As I steered back onto the blacktop I filed for future reference his amazing statement that a grand or two, maybe more, was of no consequence.

VI

THE *Monroe County Register,* eight pages, was published in Timberburg once a week, on Friday afternoon, and copies of it arrived at Vawter's in Lame Horse around five o'clock. At the cabin we were usually willing to wait until Saturday to get our copy, or even Monday or Tuesday, but that Friday I was at Vawter's when it came, not by accident, and I got two extra copies. At five-thirty Wolfe and I were in his room discussing an item on the front page which said:

JESSUP PUTS NERO WOLFE
ON HUCKLEBERRY MURDER CASE

Famous New York Sleuth
to Probe Slaying
of Philip Brodell

(Special Exclusive)

County Attorney Thomas R. Jessup announced today that he has arranged with Nero Wolfe, the internationally known private detective, and his confidential assistant, Archie Goodwin, to act as special investigators in the inquiry into the murder of Philip Brodell of St. Louis, a guest at the ranch of William T. Farnham, near Lame Horse, on July 25th.

Asked by a *Register* reporter if he expected Wolfe and Goodwin to get evidence that would strengthen the case against Harvey Greve, who is in the county jail charged

with the murder, Jessup said, "Not specifically or neces-
sarily. If I considered the case against Greve to be weak he
wouldn't have been charged and held without bail. It is simply that I learned that Nero Wolfe was available, and this
case has aroused intense and nation-wide interest, and I felt
that the people of Monroe County, the people of the en-
tire State of Montana, would expect me to use the services of
such an outstanding investigator as Nero Wolfe if that was
possible, and it was."

The county attorney added, "Wolfe and Goodwin will of
course be under my supervision and control. There will
be no additional expense to the county, since they ask no
fee, and any evidence they secure will be scrutinized and
checked by my office. If they find no new evidence no harm
will be done. If they do find new evidence, and my office
finds it to be valid and material, I think the people of Monroe County will agree with me that they have rendered us a
service."

Asked if he was aware that it is generally known that
Archie Goodwin, who is a guest at the cabin of Miss Lily
Rowan, owner of the Bar JR Ranch, has been trying to find
evidence that would weaken the case against Greve, not
strengthen it, the county attorney stated that the personal
opinion or interest of Archie Goodwin, or of anyone else,
would not be permitted to affect the performance of his duty.

"What I want," he said, "and what the people of Monroe
County want, is the truth, the whole truth, and nothing but
the truth."

Asked by a *Register* reporter if he had been consulted
about the entry of Wolfe and Goodwin into the investigation, Sheriff Morley Haight said, "No comment." Further
questions got the same reply. "No comment."

Nero Wolfe, reached by telephone at Miss Rowan's cabin,
where he is also a guest, would say only that he would say

nothing because he thought it proper that all information about his participation in the case should come only from County Attorney Jessup.

Word of this development came just as we were preparing to go to press, and we're giving ourselves a pat on the back at being the first paper in the country to get it into type. It isn't often a weekly gets a national scoop. We're sending five copies of this edition to the Library of Congress. Hang onto yours. It may be worth money some day.

Reading it, Wolfe had made a face several times, but in our discussion of it he had criticized only two words. He said "sleuth" was a vulgarism, and "supervision" was jugglery. But he admitted that everybody knows that if an elected person means everything he says he's a damn fool, so there was no argument.

There had been an argument the previous evening when Jessup had phoned to say he had decided that it would be in the public interest to accept our offer to assist him in the investigation, and we could get our credentials at his office at eleven o'clock in the morning, and Wolfe had said I would go for them. I was a little surprised that Jessup hadn't said that Wolfe must come too, but probably he was afraid that he would try to talk him into letting us go through the file, which hadn't been mentioned. The argument had come afterward between Wolfe and me. I had said that my first stop after getting the credentials would be the Presto filling station for some conversation with Gil Haight, and he said no, and I said that aside from the chance of starting something I wanted the satisfaction of seeing his face when I flashed the credentials on him.

"No," Wolfe repeated, emphatic. "His alibi can be attacked only through the men who support it, and that can wait until there is nothing better to do."

"For me," I said, "there's nothing better to do than telling Gilbert Haight I've got some questions and asking him if he would prefer to go to the county attorney's office to answer them. So that's what I'll do."

. "I said no."

"But I say yes, and the question is what *I* do."

A confrontation. Our eyes were meeting. Mine were just the eyes of a friendly equal who knew he had a point so there was no use squabbling, but his were narrowed to slits. He closed them long enough for a couple of good deep breaths, then opened them to normal. "This is the eighth of August," he said. "Thursday."

"Right."

"Your vacation ended Wednesday, July thirty-first. As you know, I brought a checkbook. Draw a check for your salary for a week and a half, which will cover it to the end of this week and put you on a weekly basis as usual."

I raised one brow, which I often find helpful because he can't do it. There were angles both pro and con. Con, I knew the people and the atmosphere and he didn't; and my taking a leave of absence without pay had been by my decision, not by agreement. Pro, his coming to get me back sooner had been by his decision, not by agreement; and while a grand or two might be of no consequence to him it was to me; and the strain of trying to remember to say please was cramping his style. It took pro about a minute to get the verdict. I figured it on a sheet from my notebook—$600 minus federal income tax withheld $153.75, state income tax $33.00, and Social Security tax $23.88—went and got the checkbook from a dresser drawer, drew a check to the order of Archie Goodwin for $389.37, and handed it to him with a pen, and he signed it and forked it over.

"Okay," I said, "instructions, please. What's better to do than riding Gil Haight?"

"I don't know." He stood up. "It's bedtime. We'll see tomorrow."

Tomorrow, Friday, the weather horned in. There on the eastern slopes of the Rockies the summer sun bats around .900. There had been only three days in July when you had to bother about a poncho when you saddled your horse. But Friday it was raining, good and steady, when I got up, when I drove to Timberburg, when I got back, late for lunch, and when I drove to Lame Horse a little before five to get the *Monroe County Register*. I don't accuse Wolfe of stalling. The credentials, which were "To Whom It May Concern" typed on Jessup's official letterhead and signed by him—one for each of us—cleared the deck, but I agreed that it was a good idea to wait until the *Register* had spread the news.

Supper was in the kitchen because it was still raining and the creek terrace was cold and clammy. Lily's copy of the *Register* was there on a shelf; presumably she had thought Mimi should know about the new status of two of the guests. The other two guests had seen it; as Wolfe and I entered the kitchen Diana, at the center table, stopped dishing her plate to look at us as if she had never seen us before, and Wade said, "Congratulations! I didn't realize you were *that* famous. When does the ball start rolling?"

I told him not until after supper because we never talked business during a meal. We had decided, after I had made the phone call to Saul, not to tell Lily about it. It would have made her uncomfortable to know that the pasts of two of her guests were being investigated by the other two, and if Saul drew a blank she needn't ever know. I was a little uncomfortable myself, sitting there passing Diana the salt or asking Wade how the outline was going, and probably Wolfe was too. That made no sense, since they knew darned well they would have been Grade A suspects if they had had any motive, but there was one chance in ten million that Saul would *not* draw a blank, and in that case there would be a behavior problem not covered by Amy Vanderbilt. Meanwhile, as we dealt with the leg of lamb, green lima beans (from the freezer), Mrs. Barnes's bread, sliced tomatoes, and huckleberry pie with coffee ice cream, I enjoyed watching Diana trying to decide if she should change her technique with us, and if so how. Evidently Wade had decided. For him we were still just fellow guests to discuss things with, like baseball (me) or structural linguistics (Wolfe).

The blaze in the fireplace in the big room had attractions on an evening like that, and the others went there with coffee, but Wolfe and I went to his room, I supposed to consider the better things to do tomorrow. But inside, instead of going to his chair by the window, he stood and asked, "Does Mr. Farnham have a telephone?"

I said yes.

"Will he have seen that newspaper?"

I said probably.

"Call him. Tell him we wish to come and discuss matters with him and anyone else available."

"In the morning?"

"Now."

I nearly said something silly. My lips parted to say, "It's raining," but I closed them before it got out. People get in ruts, including me. Many a time I had known him to postpone sending me on an errand if the weather was bad, and it took something very special, like a chance to get a specimen of a new orchid, to get him out of the house in rain or snow. But evidently this was extra special—getting back home as soon as possible—and, saying nothing, I went down the hall to the big room and across to the table where the phone was, and dialed a number, and after four rings a voice said hello.

"Bill? Archie Goodwin."

"Oh, hello again. I see you've got a badge."

"Not a badge, just a piece of paper. Apparently you've seen the *Register*."

"I sure have. You *and* Nero Wolfe. Now the fur will start to fly, huh?"

"Maybe. We hope so. Mr. Wolfe and I would like to drop in for a little talk with you and yours—everybody that's around—if it's convenient. Especially Sam Peacock. A good way to pass a rainy evening."

"Why especially Sam?"

"The man who found the body is always special. But the others too—naturally Mr. Wolfe wants to meet the people who saw the most of Brodell. Okay?"

"Sure, why not? Mr. DuBois was just saying he would like to meet him. Come ahead."

He hung up. Lily, with Diana and Wade, was over by the fireplace with her back to it, watching television, and when I asked if we could take the car to run up to Farnham's she said of course with no question or comment, and I went to my room for ponchos.

I had never seen Wolfe in a hooded poncho of any color, and the ones Lily stocked were bright red. They were all the same size, barely big enough to take his dimensions, but even so he looked very gay—leaving out his face, which was pretty grim. It was still grim when, leaving the car under the firs at Farnham's, we splashed around to the front, with a flashlight to spot puddles, and I opened the screen door and knocked on the solid one, which was closed. It was opened by William T. Farnham.

And, after shaking hands with Farnham and getting his help with the poncho, Wolfe put on an act. He always welcomed a chance to show off, but there it served two other purposes: impressing the audience and avoiding shaking so many hands. Besides Farnham there were six people in the room: three men and a woman around a card table over near the fireplace, and two men standing, kibitzing. Wolfe walked over, stopped four paces away, and said, "Good evening. I have been told of you by Mr. Goodwin." He nodded at the woman. "Mrs. Amory."

At the man across from her—round-faced, wide-browed, with his balding process well started: "Dr. Robert Amory, from Seattle."

At the man at her left—late thirties, broad-shouldered, square-jawed, needing a shave: "Mr. Joseph Colihan, from Denver."

At the man at her right—middle forties, foreign-looking, dark skin, bushy eyebrows: "Mr. Armand DuBois, also from Denver."

At the man standing behind Amory—nudging sixty, rough weathered skin, thick gray hair, in working Levi's and a pink shirt with a tear on one shoulder: "Mr. Bert Magee."

At the man standing back of Colihan, farther off—around thirty, thin scrawny neck, thin bony face, undersized—also in Levi's, with a shirt that looked like dirty leather, and a red and white neck rag: "Mr. Sam Peacock."

Farnham, there after disposing of the ponchos, said, "Now I call that a roundup." Of the six men present, not counting Wolfe and me, he was the only one I would have called handsome—rugged outdoors open-spaces handsome. He asked Wolfe, "How about some wet cheer? Anything from Montana Special to coyote piss, if I've got it."

"He drinks beer," Armand DuBois said.

Wolfe asked, "What's Montana Special?"

"Any open moving water but rainwater. Creek or river. Good for you either plain or diluted, but in weather like this it's better diluted with gargle. Name it. Beer?"

"Nothing now, thank you. Perhaps later. As you know, Mr. Goodwin and I have a job to do. But we're interrupting a game."

"Bridge isn't a game," DuBois said, "it's a brawl. We've been at it all day." He pushed his chair back and rose. "We would much rather hear you ask questions, at least I would."

"I hear you're tough," Farnham said, "but you don't look tough. Of course like the dude said to the bronc, you can't always tell by appearances. Do you want us one at a time or in a herd?"

"One at a time would take all night," Wolfe said. "We are officially accredited, but we came to inquire, not to harass. Shall we sit?"

They moved. There were two long roomy couches at right angles to the fireplace, and DuBois and Farnham took the card table and chairs away. Knowing that Wolfe would share a couch with others only if there was no alternative, I brought a chair that would take him and put it at the end of the couches, facing the fireplace, and one for me. They got distributed—Farnham, Peacock, Magee, and Colihan on the couch at our left, and DuBois and the Amorys on the one at the right. As she sat, Mrs. Amory said to Wolfe, "I'm trying to think of something you can ask *me*. I'm closer to tight than I've been for years after this rainy day and I want to see what I'd say." She put a hand to her mouth to cover what might have been a burp. "I *think* I'd make something up."

"I advise against it, madam. Mr. Goodwin has informed me thoroughly." Wolfe sent his eyes around. "I know, from Mr. Goodwin, how each of you spent that Thursday after-noon—what he has been told. I know that all of you, except Mrs. Amory, think it likely that Mr. Greve killed that man. Mr. Goodwin and I think he didn't. Mr. Jessup, the county attorney, knows that, but he also knows that we don't intend to try to concoct evidence to support our opinion; we intend only to find it if it exists, and the best place to start is here, with those closest to Mr. Brodell during his last three days and nights. First, Mr. Farnham, a point you can cover best. As you know, no bullets were found, but the nature of the wounds indicated the kind of gun that fired the shots. You own such a gun?"

"Sure I do. So do a lot of other people."

"Where is yours kept?"

"In a closet in my room."

"Is it accessible? Is the closet locked?"

"No."

"Is the gun usually loaded?"

"Of course not. Nobody keeps a gun loaded."

"Is ammunition accessible?"

"Yes. Naturally. A gun's no good without ammunition. On a shelf in the closet."

"Was there, that Thursday, any other gun on your premises—to your knowledge?"

"None that could have done that to Brodell's shoulder and neck. I've got two shotguns and a revolver, and Bert Magee has a shotgun, but that's all."

"You told Mr. Goodwin that you and Mrs. Amory spent that afternoon on horseback on what is called the Upper Berry Creek trail. Is that correct?"

"Yes."

"*Most* of the afternoon?"

"All of it from two o'clock on."

"Then you don't know how your gun spent the afternoon. Anyone could have taken it and used it and put it back. When you next saw it, was it precisely as you had left it?"

"Balls." Farnham's voice was raised. "If you ask me, you're a lousy investigator. If I say yes, it was, then you say the only way I could know it was would be if I went and looked when I knew about Brodell, and if I did that I must have thought that someone that belongs here shot him. You're not tough, you're just half-assed tricky." He got up and took a step. "You might as well beat it. These folks are my guests and my men, and we don't have to take your brand of crap. Drag it."

Wolfe's shoulders went up an eighth of an inch and down again. "I thought it preferable," he said, "both for you and for us, to do it this way. To summon you to the county attorney's office as material witnesses, probably singly, would be a nuisance for me and an inconvenience for you. If you resent my implying that one of the people in this room might have killed Mr. Brodell you're a nincompoop. Why else would I come here in a downpour? I said I came to inquire, not to harass, but inquiries about homicide are rarely bland. Shall we go on, here and now, or not?"

"That's not crap, Bill," DuBois said. "We all think Greve probably killed him, all but Mrs. Amory, but Nero Wolfe is not a gump. As I've said before, it seemed to me that the sheriff could have been a little more curious about your gun. He didn't even look at it."

"Yes he did." Farnham was still on his feet. "The next day. Friday afternoon."

"Well, *that* was lousy investigating. Sit down and cool it." DuBois turned to Wolfe. "Do me while he counts ten. Joe Colihan and I were across the river that afternoon with Bert Magee, climbing mountains, so we alibi each other, but we're close friends and he'd lie for me any day. Harass me. I'll try to stick it."

"Later," Wolfe said. "I haven't finished with Mr. Farnham." He tilted his head to look up at him. "We can dispose of the gun, for now, with one question. Did you at any time, after Mr. Brodell's body was found, thinking it conceivable that your gun had been used, go and look at it and the supply of ammunition?"

"Of course I did." Farnham sat down. "That night. Anyone with any sense would. To see if it was there. It was, and it hadn't been fired, and no ammunition was gone."

Wolfe nodded. "I don't ask if, when the possibility that your gun had been used entered your mind, the name of an individual entered with it. You would say no, and only you know what happened inside your skull. I do ask: during the three days that Mr. Brodell was here alive had there been any noticeable conflict between him and anyone else?"

"No."

"Oh for God's sake, Bill." Joseph Colihan's high-pitched voice didn't go with his broad shoulders and square jaw. "The man wants the facts." To Wolfe: "Brodell and I had some words the day he got here. Monday. I had been here two weeks and I was riding the horse he had had last year, and he wanted it, and I liked it. When I went out Tuesday morning he had his saddle on it, and I took it off, and he tried to stop me. He swung a bridle at me and skinned my ear with the bit, and I roughed him up a little. After that we didn't speak, but I kept the horse, so I didn't have to shoot him. Anyway I'm not a hunter and I wouldn't know how to load Farnham's gun. I didn't even know he had one."

"Neither did I," DuBois said, "but of course I can't prove it."

"Had either of you had any previous contact with Mr. Brodell?"

They both said no. Wolfe's eyes went to the right. "Had you, Dr. Amory? Had you ever seen Mr. Brodell before he arrived that Monday?"

"I had not." Amory's deep full voice would have been just right for Colihan.

"Had you, Mrs. Amory?"

"No."

He stayed at her. "What was your opinion of him?"

"Of Philip Brodell?"

"Yes."

"Well . . . I could make something up for *that* because you can't see inside my skull either. But I'm on your side, you know. I don't think anyone here killed him, why would they, but I'm rooting for you. My opinion of him—you see, we knew he was coming, and we knew he was the father of that girl's baby, so I had an idea of him before I saw him. You know how a woman's mind works."

"I do not. No one does. Why are you rooting for me?"

"Oh, they're all so cocksure about it. A he-man father and his daughter's honor, hurray. As for Philip Brodell, I was so busy trying to see what he had that had made it so easy for him to seduce that girl—I suppose you know everybody thought she was what they call a *good* girl—that I don't really know what my *opinion* was. Anyway it wouldn't help you any, would it?"

"It might if I could get it. One possibility that has been suggested to Mr. Goodwin is that Mr. Brodell seduced *you,* and your husband learned of it and removed him. That has the attraction that he has no alibi."

The Amorys had both made noises. His was a scornful grunt, and hers was an amused snort. "Of course," she said, "the Greve girl would suggest that. Naturally. I *doubt* if he could have seduced me in three years. But in three days?" She looked at me. "Why didn't you ask me?"

"I was deciding how to put it," I said. "The suggestion didn't come from Miss Greve."

"I am aware," Amory told Wolfe, "that anyone remotely involved in a murder investigation must expect impertinences and absurdities, but we don't have to encourage them. I covered some ten miles up the river that afternoon, and I had no gun, and my wife was with Mr. Farnham, as you know. Neither of us has any knowledge of anything that could possibly be relevant. I live in another state, but investigating procedure is basically the same everywhere in the West, and I'd like to know how you fit in. If a law officer asks ridiculous questions a citizen might as well answer them and get rid of him, but why you? If you told the county attorney something that made him think that man Greve may not be guilty, you should tell us if you expect us to respect your authority. Why did he give you official standing?"

"Disaster insurance," Wolfe said.

"Insurance? Against what?"

"Against the possibility of a demonstration that I deserve my reputation. You must know, Dr. Amory, that the validity of a reputation depends on its nature. The renown of a champion runner or discus thrower has a purely objective basis—the recordings of stopwatches or tape measures. Consider your own profession. The renown of a practicing physician is partly objective—how many of the people he treats get well and how many die—but there are other factors that can't be objectively measured. A doctor who has many patients and is trusted and well regarded by them may be disdained by his colleagues. With a professional investigator, his public repute may have very little objective foundation, if any; his admired feats could have resulted exclusively from luck. Take me. Fewer than a dozen people are qualified to say if my reputation has been fairly earned."

"Archie Goodwin is," DuBois said.

"Yes, he's qualified, but he's biased. An *ex parte* judgment is always suspect." Wolfe's eyes went right and left. "Mr. Jessup was well advised to facilitate my inquiry by giving me a lever. Sensibly, he didn't try to insist on knowing why Mr. Goodwin and I reject the plerophory that Mr. Greve is a murderer; he knew we would reserve our grounds until we had impressive evidence. As for this conversation, our coming here for some talk, we're not so naïve as to suppose that anything could be learned by asking you routine questions. Mutual alibis among possible culprits are ignored by a competent investigator. Mr. DuBois. You invited me to harass you. If I do it won't be by inane questions."

His eyes took them in again. "There was the chance that meeting you here, together, would give us a hint of frictions that might be fruitful. It's difficult for five people to live under one roof for three days without getting the skins of their egos scratched. I needed to decide if I should take the time and trouble to spend hours with each of you, *tête-à-tête*, reviewing every minute, every word spoken, during the three days Mr. Brodell was with you. I doubt it. If, for instance, Mr. Colihan or Dr. Amory heard a comment by one of you, or saw a gesture, suggestive of more knowledge of Mr. Brodell than had been disclosed, would he tell me? I doubt it. I have seen no indication of animus that would move any of you to risk such involvement. If one of you had previous contact with Mr. Brodell, evidence of it probably won't be found here. It may be necessary to go to St. Louis, his home, or send someone. I hope not."

"I wouldn't object to spending hours with you *tête-à-tête*," DuBois said. "Any time you say."

"Neither would I," Mrs. Amory said. "If you—"

"By God, I would," Farnham blurted. "If you ask me, you're just a jawbox. The sooner you go to St. Louis the better. All right, you've met us. The door's over there."

Wolfe nodded at him. "It's probably only your temperament, but it could be apprehension of what I might expose. Before I leave I must talk with the one man who may say something helpful. But first, Mr. Magee, a routine question for you. You were with Mr. DuBois and Mr. Colihan across the river that Thursday afternoon?"

Bert Magee nodded. "That's right."

"All afternoon? Continuously?"

"Yep."

"What time did you get back here?"

"Six o'clock, just about."

"You know what I'm after: something, anything, to support my assumption that it wasn't Mr. Greve who shot that man. Can you help me?"

"Nope. Of course Harvey should've shot him, and he did, and I hope they turn him loose."

"That's humane but not civilized. Mr. Peacock. I have many questions for you, mostly routine, because I understand you are best equipped to answer them. You were often with Mr. Brodell during those three days?"

Sam Peacock looked even smaller than he was, between those two huskies, Farnham on his right and Magee on his left, and the red and white bandanna didn't hide his scrawny neck, it called attention to it. His squinty gray eyes darted a glance at Farnham before they went to Wolfe. "Uhuh," he said. "I guess you could say often. Last year I gave him a fly that got him a six-pound rainbow, and that made me turtle feathers. When he came this year Bill sent me to Timberburg to get him, and the first thing he said, he wanted to know if I had another one corralled."

"What time did he arrive that Monday?"

"He got to Timberburg on the noon bus, but he had to scare up a pile of things, duds and tackle and I don't know what all, so we didn't get here until . . . I guess it was . . . what time was it, Bill?"

"Around five," Farnham said.

"Maybe. I would have said a little later."

"Were you present when he met the others? Dr. and Mrs. Amory and Mr. DuBois and Mr. Colihan?"

"No sir, I wasn't. I guess I was in the kitchen eating supper with Bert. After supper Phil asked me to go to the river with him, and I didn't have to, but I didn't want to say no, so I went."

"You called him by his first name?"

"Uhuh. He asked me to even before he got the rainbow. Some do and some don't."

"Were you with him on Tuesday?"

"Yes sir, I was." Peacock sent a glance at Colihan. His tongue was slow but his eyes were quick. "That was the morning there was some trouble about the Monty horse. Phil told me to saddle him and I did, and here comes Mr. Colihan, and like he told you, they mixed it some. So I went to the corral and got Teabag for Phil, and we went downriver byyond the flats. All day, we made it back just in time for supper. Phil and the Teabag horse didn't get along any too good, but I guess I'm telling you more than you want to know. Anyway I told Archie all this."

Wolfe nodded. "Sometimes he's careless about details. You couldn't tell me more than I want to know. Did you see Mr. Brodell after supper Tuesday?"

"No sir, I didn't. He was played out and anyway I wasn't here. I was off and around."

"The next day? Wednesday?"

"Uhuh, that was better. Phil and me left early and went upriver on two laigs apiece. He didn't get no six-pound rainbow, but he filled a big creel and it was a real good day any way you look at it. Up at the falls he slipped on a rock and got dunked, but the sun soon dried him and no bones was broke. Of course he was draggin' his ass by the time we saw the chimney smoke comin' in, and his back hadn't forgot the day he had spent on Teabag, so when I asked him what he had in mind for the next day he said the way he felt right then he might not get out of bed even for meals. But he did. Next morning Connie told me he had stowed away a stack of ulcer patches and three fish for breakfast."

"Who is Connie?"

"She's the cook."

"He was with you Thursday morning?"

"No sir, he wasn't. He said he was goin' to mosey over for a look at Berry Creek and I would set too fast a pace. Then after lunch he said—"

"If you please. How long was he gone in the morning?"

"I'd say two hours, maybe more. Then after—"

"Did he go up Berry Creek, or down?"

"If he said, I didn't listen. It's an easy trail over to the bend and then up or down, take your pick. I'd say he didn't go up to the pool because he didn't take tackle."

"Did he mention meeting anyone?"

"No sir, he didn't." Peacock tugged at a corner of the neck rag. "You got a lot of questions, mister."

"I once asked a woman ten thousand questions. That Thursday morning is of interest because apparently it was the only time Mr. Brodell was off alone—except the afternoon. The easy trail to the creek—is it near the road at any point?"

"Uhuh. Where it circles around to miss a climb."

"So he may not have got to the creek, if he met someone on the road. You spoke with him when he returned?"

"Not when he returned. After lunch."

"Did you gather from what he said that he had been to the creek?"

"I don't do much gatherin' from what a man says. Now if he said he saw a fourteen-inch Dolly Varden in the pool above the bend you might say he had been to the creek, but you got to figure maybe he did and maybe he didn't. A man can say things like that just because it sounds good. Anyhow we didn't talk much after lunch. I was out by the corral trimmin' a post and he comes and says he was goin' up the ridge to get some berries. That was at five minutes after three. Connie says it was five after when he left the house, but I keep my watch right." He looked at his wrist. "Right now it's nine minutes to ten."

"And you didn't see him again—alive?"

"No sir, I didn't."

"Where were you the next five hours?"

"I was around. It took a while to get that post in and then there was a loose shoe on a horse, and a saddle had to have a new cinch, and some other little things."

"You didn't leave the premises?"

"Now that's quite a word, that 'premises.' If you mean did I go up the ridge with a gun and shoot Phil, no sir, I didn't. That wasn't on my program. Any time Connie had opened the door and yelled for me she'd 'a' got me."

"And you saw no one with a gun?"

"That's correct. That's a fair statement. The first man I saw was Bill when he come in with Mrs. Amory and I took the horses. I was in my room washin' up when Bert and his two got in. Right after supper Bill asked me again about Phil but I couldn't tell him any more than I already had. When the sun was gone we thought we'd better look around and Bill and Bert and me went up the ridge. I knew the spots Phil liked better than they did, so it was me that found him."

Wolfe turned his head to look at me. His unasked question was, "Has he varied any, with the others present, from what he told you, and if so, do you challenge him now?" I shook my head and said, "Nothing to add, even with credentials."

He sent his eyes around and told a barefaced lie. "I suppose I should intermit. Before proceeding beyond this preamble I must consult Mr. Jessup; as he said, the inquiry is under his supervision and control. I think it quite likely that at least one of you is withholding material facts, but I doubt if prolonging this through the night would disclose them.

An obvious point: you have all been placed, provision-
ally, for that Thursday afternoon, but where were you that
morning during the two hours when Mr. Brodell was off
alone?"

He shook his head. "I don't want to send Mr. Goodwin to
St. Louis, I need him here, but we shall see." He got to his
feet. "It's astonishing how frequently grown men, apparently
sane, get the notion that they can conceal facts that are
easily ascertainable. I'll bear in mind, Mr. DuBois, that you
have invited harassment, and I may oblige you."

He moved, and so did I, across to the rack in an alcove for
the ponchos and flashlight. They all stayed put, but as I was
pulling my hood over, here came Farnham to the rack, and he
got a poncho and put it on and went and opened the door.
It was pretty late in the day for him to be getting polite, and
I supposed he was going out for some little errand, but he
came across to the car with us. The rain had let up but there
was plenty of drip from the firs. Farnham opened the door
of the station wagon for Wolfe to get in, and then he held
it open and did his little errand. He spoke. "I don't want
you to get the idea that I have tried to conceal any facts.
Some facts are other people's business and some aren't. I
don't think anybody around here knows that Phil Brodell's
father has got a mortgage on my place and there's no reason
why they should, but if Goodwin goes to St. Louis and sees
Brodell, of course that's one fact he'll get, and you might
as well get it from me."

Wolfe grunted. "A substantial mortgage?"

"Goddammit, yes!" He slammed the door shut harder than
necessary.

VII

AT A QUARTER PAST TEN Saturday morning I opened a door on the first floor of the Monroe County courthouse in Timberburg and entered—a door with a glass panel that had painted on it in big bold black gilt-edged letters:

MORLEY HAIGHT

SHERIFF

Inside, not even turning my head for a glance at the county employee seated at a table inside the railing, I kept going, on through the gate in the railing, across to a door in the left wall, opened it, and stepped in.

I admit it wouldn't be correct to say I was in pursuit of a fugitive from justice, but the man I had had in tow had broken loose, and it would have been a pleasure to bulldog him. I had not been cocky. Arriving at the Presto gas station twenty minutes ago, at 9:55, I had pulled over to the edge of the gravel, got out, asked the help politely if Gil was around, and gone where his thumb pointed, on through the bright sun to the shady inside. Gilbert Haight, over to the left, stacking cans of oil on a shelf, twisted his long neck for a look at me, twisted it back to see his hands place a couple of cans nice and even, turned around, and said, "Nice mahrnin'."

If it had been yesterday instead of today and I had just come from Jessup's office with the credentials, I would have

had a little fun, but now it was just a job. "Better than yesterday," I said. "That was quite a rain."

"It sure was."

"Maybe we could sit somewhere for a little talk?"

He nodded. "I knew you'd be comin'."

"Naturally. If your father still says you mustn't talk to me
maybe I should see him first. I wouldn't mind."

"I bet you wouldn't. He don't say that. He says the law's
the law. He knows the law. But this is no place to talk, people
comin' and goin'. I suppose you've got some kind of a paper
from the county attorney."

I got an envelope from a pocket, took from it the "To
Whom It May Concern," unfolded it, and handed it to him.
He read it twice, taking his time, handed it back, and said,
"It looks legal to me. I guess the best place to talk is right
there in his office, where it sure will be legal. My sister's got
my car so we'll go in yours. Miss Rowan's."

I could have said something like "Father knows best,"
but didn't bother. He put a few more cans in place, went out
and told his colleague he was leaving for a while—his priv-
ilege, since his father owned the place—and came and joined
me on the front seat of the station wagon. It was only half
a mile to the courthouse. As usual on a Saturday morning
all the nearby parking spots were occupied, but I turned in,
swung around the courthouse to the rear, and on past a sign
that said OFFICIAL CARS ONLY. One, I was now official, and
two, his name was Haight. The rear door of the courthouse
was standing open, and I led the way in and headed down
the long hall to the front, where the main stairs were. We
passed doors on both sides, but the three on the left were
crisscrossed with iron bars because that was the old part of
the county jail. Entering the big lobby, I turned right toward
the stairs, but halfway there I stopped and wheeled because
I no longer had company. He had headed back toward the

opening to a side hall and was turning into it on the trot.
I had no desire to stop him but wanted to know, not just
guess, so I got to the hall fast, in time to see him open a door
and go in—and as I said, the door was shut when I reached
it.

The county employee at the table barked something and
jumped up as I crossed, quick, to the inner door and on in.
I stopped short of the desk and said, "What the hell, as long
as it's legal."

You haven't met Sheriff Morley Haight, which is fair
enough, because he hadn't met himself. Lily and I, having
had occasion to discuss him, had done so. His basic idea of a
Western sheriff was Wyatt Earp, so that was how he dressed,
but obviously the modern way to tote a gun was on a belt
like a state trooper's, so he did, though he knew he shouldn't.
An even bigger difficulty was that he was a born loudmouth,
a natural roof-raiser, and of course that wouldn't do at all
for a Wyatt Earp. As if that wasn't enough, he had told vari-
ous people, two of whom I had met, that when there was a
problem to handle he always asked himself what J. Edgar
Hoover would do. The product was a personality mess that
couldn't have been made any worse even by a trained psy-
choanalyst.

Since he had known what I would do as soon as he heard
about my credentials from Jessup, and since he had told his
son what to do, my marching in was no surprise for him and
he didn't pretend it was. He just squinted at me, his Wyatt
Earp squint, and growled, "What kept you?"

His son Gil, who was standing over by a tier of filing cabi-
nets, had got his long-limbed setup, including his extra inch
and a half of neck, straight from Dad, and of course that
wasn't ideal for a sheriff, but he had got elected anyway and
that's the test—lick your handicaps. One of his dodges was

keeping his shoulders up and back to make them look
broader, and he was doing that now.

There was a plain wood chair at the end of his desk, and
I went and took it. "Mr. Wolfe thought there were better
things to do yesterday," I said politely. "This will be the first
time I ever questioned a murder suspect with a sheriff
listening. Do we want a stenographer?"

"We don't need one." He opened a desk drawer, fingered
in it, brought papers out, and selected one. "Here's an extra
copy of a signed statement by one of the suspects *I* questioned." He held it out and I took it. "I guess you can read?"

I didn't bother to bat that back. The exhibit was typewrit-
ten on a plain 8½-by-11 sheet, single-spaced and wide-mar-
gined:

Timberburg, Montana
July 27, 1968

I, Gilbert Haight, living at 218 Jefferson Street, Timberburg, Montana, hereby state that on Thursday, July 25,
1968, I was at the Presto Gas Station on Main Street continuously from 12:50 p.m. to 2:25 p.m. The times given in
this statement are exact within five minutes, and are all
for the aforesaid Thursday, July 25.

From 2:35 p.m. to 4:25 p.m., continuously, I was with
Miss Bessie Boughton at her home at 360 Willow Street,
Timberburg. From 4:40 p.m. to 5:05 p.m., continuously,
I was with Mr. Homer Dowd at his place of business, the
Dowd Roofing Company, on Main Street, Timberburg.
From 5:20 p.m. to 6:00 p.m., continuously, I was with
Mr. Jimmy Negron at his chicken farm on Route 27 south
of Timberburg.

Gilbert Haight

Witness: Effie T. Duggers

The names were typed below the signatures. Apple-pie
order.

Of course he expected me either to tackle Gil on the alibi, trying to find a crack, or to get personal with him about his relations with Alma Greve and his contacts with Philip Brodell, so I had to do something else. There weren't many alternatives. I folded the document carefully, pocketed it, narrowed my eyes at him, and said the way Wyatt Earp would have said it, "That seems to account for him, subject to a check, but what about you? Where were you from two p.m. to six p.m. on Thursday, July twenty-fifth?"

The reaction was even better than expected. His hand went to his belt and for a half a second I thought he was actually going to draw; his eyes bugged; and he roared like a bull at the touch of the branding iron, "You goddam New York punk!" He then jerked his chair back and started up, but I don't know how fast or far he came because I was walking out and my back was turned. On through the anteroom and down the hall and out to the car.

Having been to 360 Willow Street once before, I didn't have to get directions. It was a neat little one-story white cottage with a narrow concrete walk leading to the three steps up to a little covered porch. I hadn't been inside because Miss Boughton had spoken her few words to me through the screen door, but this time she pushed it open and I entered. Obviously she too had been expecting me, though she didn't say so. All she said, after inviting me in and taking me to a neat little room with two windows, and one wall covered nearly to the ceiling with shelves of books, was that I should have phoned because she often spent weekends at her brother's ranch. Before she sat on the biggest chair of the three available she had to pick up an embroidery frame with work in progress that was there on the seat. Probably the Thomas Jefferson that decorated the back of my chair had come from that frame.

"I had Gilbert Haight in my political-science class for two

years," she said. "When I started teaching thirty-eight years ago, they called it history."

I gave her a cordial smile. Evidently we weren't going to bother about approach, but I asked if she would like to see my credentials from the county attorney.

She shook her head, making glints dart at me as the light from a window bounced from the thick lenses of her gold-rimmed cheaters, which were too big for her little round face. "Gilbert saw it," she said. "He just told me on the phone. Of course it wouldn't have been proper for me to talk when you were here before, since you were just a stranger I knew nothing about, but now I'll be glad to. Some people are criticizing Tom Jessup for getting outsiders like Nero Wolfe and you to help, but that's parochial and narrow-minded. I thoroughly approve. Tom's a good boy, I had him back in nineteen forty-three, a war year. We are all citizens of this great Republic, and it's your Constitution just as much as it's mine. What do you want to know?"

"Just a few little facts," I said. "Since you teach political science of course you know that when a crime is committed, for instance homicide, anyone with a known motive is asked some questions, and his answers should be checked. Gilbert Haight says he was here with you for part of a certain afternoon a couple of weeks ago. So of course he was. Right?"

"Yes. He came about half past two and left about half past four."

"What day of the week was it?"

"It was a Thursday. Thursday, July twenty-fifth."

"How sure are you it was *that* day?"

Her lips parted to show two even rows of little white teeth. I wouldn't have called it a grin, but she probably thought it was. "I suppose," she said, "there is no man or woman anywhere who has answered more questions than I have in the last thirty-eight years. You get so you know exactly what

questions to expect, and I decided the best way to answer
that one would be to tell you the whole thing. When I heard
the next day about that man being shot I said to myself, 'Now
Gilbert won't have to tar and feather him.' "

"Oh," I said.

She nodded and I got more glints. "You probably want to
know why he was here two whole hours that day. It took that
long to persuade him. I won't say he looks on me as his
mother—he was only four years old when his mother died
—because I'm not cut out to be a mother, I'm too intellec-
tual, but I'm not bragging when I say that Gilbert isn't the
only boy who has come to me for advice when he had a problem. He had told me all about *that* problem—that girl he
wanted to marry, and that man. When he came here that
day he was all worked up because the man had come back
and he had decided he had to do something but didn't know
what. The first thing he asked me, he wanted my advice how
he could force him to marry her."

"He must have a shotgun."

"Of course, every boy has a shotgun, but the trouble was
more her than the man. With her it was double trouble. One
trouble was Gilbert still wanted to marry her himself, and
the other was that she was saying that she hated Philip Brodell and never wanted to see him again. So I told him he
didn't need anybody's advice on that because he couldn't
take it, no matter what it was. Even if he could somehow
force *him,* there was no possible way he could force *her,* and
on top of that, if he still wanted to marry her himself, where
would he be if she had a husband? I told him he wasn't thinking it through. I always tell my boys and girls the *first* thing
to learn is to think things through. George Washington did
and John Adams did and Abraham Lincoln did."

"And you do."

"I certainly try to. So then he proposed another idea. Did

you know that more than ninety per cent of the duels fought
in this country took place west of the Mississippi?"

"If you mean on television, yes."

"I don't mean television, I mean *history*. I have re-
searched it. They didn't call them duels, but that's what they
were, and they didn't happen often until our forefathers got
west of that river. It's an important historical fact, and my
boys and girls are always interested in it. I don't think . . ."
She shut her eyes and compressed her lips.

She opened her eyes and went on. "I was trying to remember if Gilbert used that word that day, 'duel.' I'm pretty
sure he didn't. He just said he would take two guns, hand
guns, and he would give one to Philip Brodell and they
would shoot it out, and he wanted my advice on the details,
how to arrange it, and where, and how many cartridges in
each gun—he said he would need only one—all the details.
Of course I had to talk him out of it."

"Why of course?"

"Well, there were several things wrong with it, but the
worst one was that historically—I mean our *Western* history
—each man used his own gun, and probably Brodell didn't
have one, and who was going to check the one Gilbert gave
him? There would have to be at least two other men in on
the preparations, and who would they be, willing to get involved in violent death like that? Because Gilbert can shoot,
and he would have killed him. So I had to talk him out of
it, but I had to suggest something else and I did."

"Let me guess. Tar and feathers."

"That's not a guess, I already told you. Tarring and feathering isn't as Western as the American duel, because it didn't
always move along with the frontier. I've never been sure it
was a good idea to give it up. If it was done by law, not just
by a mob, and if you want a penalty to be *effective,* especially as a deterrent, tarring and feathering would be better

than a fine or a month in jail. Wouldn't you think twice before you'd risk being tarred and feathered?"

"I think twice before I risk a fine. Tarring and feathering, three times at least."

She nodded and the glints came. "The way it looked to me, the main point was to get that man away from here, so he would *stay* away, and if he was tarred and feathered, that should do it. Gilbert tried to argue that it wouldn't settle anything, but that was just talk, he really liked the idea because the one thing he couldn't stand was the man coming back. He knew he was back ten minutes after he got off the bus that Monday. Some friend told him. You have friends like that, we all have. We decided he would need eight or ten boys to help him—he said he could get as many as he wanted —and the best time would be Saturday night at Lame Horse because Brodell would almost certainly be there, at Woody's. I suppose you know about Saturday nights at Woody's."

"Yes."

"We decided all the details—where to get the tar and feathers."

"Homer Dowd and Jimmy Negron."

Her chin jerked up and she frowned. "You knew all about it." From her tone, she would have sent me to the principal's office if it had been handy.

Not wanting to leave under a cloud, I explained. "No, I only knew where he said he went when he left here—to the Dowd Roofing Company and Negron's chicken farm, but I didn't know why." I rose. "So he was completely sold on tar and feathers?"

"He wasn't *sold*. He didn't have to be. He just realized it was the best solution for his problem. Are you going? I haven't told you much. All I've done, you asked me how sure I was it was *that* day, and I told you. What else do you want to know?"

"I want to know who shot Philip Brodell." I sat down. "You said Gilbert—I'll quote it—you said, 'He had told me all about *that* problem, that girl he wanted to marry and that man.' If you can spare the time I would appreciate it if you'll tell me everything he told you about Brodell."

"Well . . . there was the question of rape. Statutory rape. She was eighteen years old. But *Gilbert* couldn't start an action."

"I know, and Mr. and Mrs. Greve didn't. But what did he say about Brodell? You may know that I don't believe Harvey Greve shot him, and I'm trying to think it through. Gilbert might have said something about him that would give me a hint."

"Not to me. I feel sorry for you, Mr. Goodwin. You have my sympathy. But I can't help you with *your* problem."

"Of course you think Harvey Greve shot him."

"Did I say I do?"

"No."

"Then don't you say it. He's innocent until a jury of his peers says he's guilty. That's one of the glories of our great Republic."

"It sure is. So are you. Citizens like you." I stood up. I wasn't exactly sore at her; it was just that a man doesn't like having a gate shut in his face any better than a horse does. I said, "I don't quite see how you fit advising him to commit assault and feathers, which is a felony, into the Constitution of our great Republic, but that's *your* problem. Think it through."

I didn't thank her for the time. I departed, not on the run, but fast enough to get outside and to the car without hearing any remarks. I pulled the car door shut and looked at both my wrist and the dash clock, a habit. Seventeen minutes past eleven. By the time I got to Main Street, only three short blocks, I had the situation analyzed. For the Dowd Roofing

Company, which was a few doors from the library, I should turn right. For the road to Lame Horse I should turn left. I turned left.

I took my time on the curves and bumps and ups-and-downs, and when I reached the end of the blacktop at Vawter's General Store it was three minutes after noon. Three o'clock Saturday afternoon in New York, and Saul might have found Manhattan so empty for the summer weekend that he had called it a day, so I pulled up in front of the Hall of Culture, went in, and got permission from Woody to use the phone. The arrangement was that Saul was not to call us unless he had something urgent; we were to call him. But all I got on two tries was no answer, so I returned to the car and headed for the cabin. In time for lunch, I thought.

There wasn't any lunch. There was no one on the terrace, and no one in the big room, or in Lily's room, or in mine, or in Wolfe's. But there were noises in the kitchen, and I found Wade there, at the can opener, opening a can of clam chowder. I asked him if it was enough for two, and he said no but there was more in the storeroom. I went and opened the small refrigerator for a survey, and got out a Boone County ham—what there was left of one. As I got a knife from a drawer I asked, "Are they all riding range?"

He was dumping the chowder into a pot. "No, they're on wheels. A car from the ranch. If I got it straight, you and Wolfe are going across to the ranch this afternoon?"

"That was the idea. Late this afternoon."

"Well, Mrs. Greve came and said she would like to give Wolfe a real Montana trout deal if she had some trout, and they collected some tackle and grub and took off for the river."

"Including Mr. Wolfe?"

"No, Lily and Diana and Mimi. And Mrs. Greve. Wolfe, I don't know. I was in my room, but I heard him in the kitchen and the storeroom around ten o'clock, so wherever he is he's not starving. Beer or coffee?"

I said neither one, thanks, I'd have milk.

We ate our snacks in the kitchen, and he probably thought my mind was wandering, because it was. It wasn't likely that Wolfe had hiked the three miles to Farnham's, to harass DuBois and others, but where was he? Worthy said there had been no phone call that he knew of, but he had been in his room. In addition to the Wolfe problem there was the Worthy problem. I had been floundering around for two full weeks and hadn't got a smell, and now Gil Haight's alibi was tight as a drum, and there I was having a bite and chatting with a man who had had both means and opportunity. Instead of a sociable chat, what I wanted to say to him was this:

"Since we're fellow guests I ought to tell you that at my request a man named Saul Panzer, who is better at almost anything than anyone else I know, is working on you in New York. If you ever had any contact there with Philip Brodell, he'll get it, so you might as well tell me now. I'm going to phone him between six and seven today and every day."

I had to use will power to keep from saying it. I wanted and needed some action, and I might get some by saying that to him. Of course if I did and there really was something that Saul could find, something good enough, it was more than possible that Worthy would no longer be around when six o'clock came, but then it would be just a chase, and that would suit me fine. But I used will power and vetoed it. Wolfe was paying me, and I was supposed to act on intelligence guided by experience only when he couldn't be consulted. So Worthy probably thought my mind was wandering.

After doing the dishes, the few we had used, he went to his room and I went outdoors. The question was how well did I know Nero Wolfe? and in two minutes I had answered it. If he had decided to do something desperate like phoning to Lame Horse or Timberburg for a car, or starting off on foot for Farnham's, he would have left a note for me and he hadn't. But he hadn't known when to expect me back from Timberburg, and he would want to know how I had made out with Gil Haight, so he wouldn't want me to roam around looking for him. Therefore I knew where he was. I went in and changed my shoes and slacks, left by the creek terrace, and started the climb. For the first few hundred yards I went right along, but when I got near the picnic spot I took it easy —not quiet enough to stalk a deer, but easy. The creek was only some thirty feet away from that rock, and along there it was fairly noisy.

He wasn't on the rock, but his coat and vest were, and a book, and a knapsack. He wasn't in sight. I advanced to the edge of the creek bank, which sloped down a little steep ten or twelve rocky feet in August, and there he was, perched on a boulder surrounded by water dancing along, his pants rolled up above his knees, his feet in the water, and the sleeves of his yellow shirt rolled up.

I said, raising my voice above the creek's noise, "You'll freeze your toes."

His head turned. "When did you get back?"

"Half an hour ago. I ate something and came straight here. Where are your cuff links?"

"In my coat pocket."

I went to the rock, lifted the coat, and found them in the right-hand pocket. Those two Muso emeralds, bigger than robin eggs, had once been in the earrings of a female who had later died and left them to Wolfe in her will. Only a year ago a man had offered him thirty-five grand for them, and I didn't want that to be added to the cost of his getting me back to New York. I put them in my pocket, and as I put his coat down I noticed that the book was *The First Circle,* by Alexander Solzhenitsyn. Not the one about Indians. I went back to the rim of the bank and said, "I met a woman who could tell you all about red men, especially the tribes west of the Mississippi River. Incidentally, she gave Gil Haight's alibi two good legs and a coat of feathers."

"Meaning?"

"Forget him."

He slid his feet around under eight inches of fast water, moved them right and left and out and back, feeling for a good spot, got upright, and faced the bank. Knowing how easy it was to take a tumble walking those loose rocks of all sizes, not only in the fast water where you couldn't see them but even on the dry bank where you could, I made it five to one that he would go down. But he didn't. He made it to a big flat slab of granite halfway up the bank, where he had left his shoes and socks, sat, and said, "Report."

"When you're up here out of danger."

"I can't put my socks on until the sun dries and warms my feet."

"You should have brought a towel." I sat, on the lip of the bank. "Verbatim?"

"If you still have the knack."

I reported. First the brief exchanges with the Haights, including Gil's signed statement, which I read, and then Bessie Boughton. I was a little rusty on word-for-word recall, having had no practice since June, and it was a pleasure to get back into the swing of it. By the time I got to the tar and feathers it was coming as smooth as a tape recorder, though the conditions were unprecedented. I had never before reported with him sitting on a slab of granite barefooted, wiggling his toes.

"So," I said, "if we get a replacement for Harvey it won't be Gilbert Haight. She has covered him good to half past

four. It's possible, better than possible, that she tells it like
it was—I beg your pardon, *as* it was—but even if she's a damn
liar she's a good one, and any jury would take it hook, line,
and feathers. But that's not the point because no jury will
ever hear it. The point is Jessup. You said he's an ass, but
is he a double-breasted ass?"

"No."

"Then we forget Gil."

"Confound it, yes."

He reached for his socks and shoes, put them on, kept a
hand on the granite slab while he got erect with a solid footing, and came on up. I didn't offer a hand because he
wouldn't have taken it, and anyway the more exercise he got
the better. As he rolled his pants and sleeves down I got the
cuff links from my pocket, and of course I had to put them
in; he couldn't very well show at the cabin with his cuffs
flapping. Not him. Then he went to the rock and got his vest
and put it on, and his coat, sat, and said, "What is a real
Montana trout deal?"

"That's a good question," I said, "and I'm sorry you asked
it." I went and sat on the other rock. "It depends on who's
cooking it, and when and where. The first real Montana trout
deal—that is, the first one cooked by a paleface—was probably at the time of the Lewis and Clark Expedition, fried
on a campfire in a rusty pan in buffalo grease, with salt if
they had any left. Since then there have been hundreds of
versions, depending on what was handy. There's an old-
timer in a hardware store in Timberburg who says that for
the real thing you rub bacon grease on a piece of brown
wrapping paper, wrap it around the trout, with the head and
tail on and plenty of salt and pepper, and put it in the oven
of a camp stove as hot as you can get it. The time depends on
the size of the trout. Mrs. Greve got her version from an
uncle of hers who was probably inspired by what he had left

at the tail end of a packing-in trip. She has changed two details: she uses aluminum foil instead of wrapping paper, and the oven of her electric range instead of a camp stove. It's very simple. Put a thin slice of ham about three inches wide on a piece of foil, sprinkle some brown sugar on it and a few little scraps of onion, and a few drops of Worcestershire sauce. Lay the trout on it, scraped and gutted but with the head and tail on, and salt it. Repeat the brown sugar and onion and Worcestershire, wrap the foil around it close, and put it in a hot oven. If some of the trout are eight or nine inches and others are fourteen or so, the timing is a problem. Serve them in the foil."

He did not scowl or growl but merely said, "It could be edible."

I nodded. "Yeah, I have noticed. You haven't said a single thing, even to me, about the feed, even the griddle cakes from a mass-produced mix or the stuff from the freezer. Obviously you gave yourself your word of honor, probably on your way to the airport, that you would take the insults to your palate without a murmur. I can hear you telling Fritz about it when we get back, assuming we do. I hope they get plenty of trout. What is your honest opinion of the canned consommé?"

I thought it would do him good to get it off his chest, but evidently he didn't. He said, "You can't go to St. Louis. You're needed here."

"Sure. To crack alibis."

"Pfui. Have you any comments about last evening?"

"None to add to the one I made on the way back, and the one you made. I still like both of them. I like the way Farnham told you about the mortgage. It could have a bearing. Then the way Sam Peacock tried to slide past that morning when Brodell went for a look at Berry Creek. You had to interrupt him twice, and when you asked if Brodell had mentioned meeting anyone he tugged at his neck rag and said you asked a lot of questions. If Brodell was alive I'd like to ask him about that Thursday morning."

"Yes. Would Mr. Peacock be available if we went there now?"

"Saturday afternoon, I doubt it."

"Will he be at that gathering at Mr. Stepanian's place this evening?"

"He always is."

"Then we'll see him there."

"We? *You're* going?"

"Yes."

My brows didn't go up; I was too impressed. I just stared.

"I'm thirsty," Wolfe said. "There are two cans of beer in the creek."

I rose and went to get them.

VIII

AT TWENTY MINUTES PAST FIVE, four of us were sharing the front room at the Greves' house with the pictures and ribbons and medals—and the silver cup and the saddle. All men. Carol Greve and Flora Eaton, the widow out of luck, were in the kitchen preparing the real Montana trout deal, which was scheduled for six o'clock. Alma was somewhere with the baby. Wolfe and I had arrived at five, and Pete Ingalls and Emmett Lake had been there expecting us, but Mel Fox had been held up by something wrong with a horse and we were waiting for him. Emmett, an old cowhand in his forties who looked the part, had said only two words, "Sit here," to me, but Pete had said a lot. From his build you would suppose his chief interest was in something that took plenty of muscle, but he was postgraduating in paleontology at the University of California, Berkeley, and this was his third summer at the Bar JR. Wolfe had asked him a question about the demonstrations at Berkeley, starting a run of remarks that would have carried us right up to suppertime if Mel Fox hadn't stopped it by joining us. Mel said he was sorry to be late and shook hands with Wolfe. He moved a chair up near mine, yanked his Levi's as he sat, a habit of his, looked at his hands, and said he hadn't even washed up. He asked if he had missed something he ought to know.

Wolfe shook his head. "We waited for you. I have been here three days, Mr. Fox, and you may have wondered why I haven't seen you sooner."

"I guess I've been too busy to do much wondering."

"I envy you. Wondering is about all I have done." Wolfe sent his eyes right and left to take them in. "Mr. Goodwin has acquainted me with you gentlemen, and if he had included any reason to suspect that one of you shot Philip Brodell I wouldn't have waited until now to speak with you. I am here in the forlorn hope that one of you knows something, unwittingly, that will supply a suggestion. To try to uncover it by asking you questions would take days. Instead, I ask you to talk. Mr. Fox, you first. Talk about Philip Brodell and his death."

"I'm not a great talker." Mel looked at me and back at Wolfe. "I've talked it out with Archie."

"I know, but let me hear you. Let your tongue go."

"Well." Mel crossed his legs. "I never traded more than twenty words with Brodell. That was one day last summer. A Sunday morning, I was at Vawter's getting some things, and he came over and said who he was and said he wanted to buy a rope to take home and it ought to be a used rope, and he wanted to know did I have one I would sell him. I told him I didn't. I guess it wasn't even twenty words. Maybe I saw him one or two other times but not to speak to, he was nothing to me. Of course he wasn't around when it came out that he was the father of Alma's baby. Then I couldn't say he was nothing to me, because Alma—well, I pulled porky quills out of her leg when she was only five years old. There was a lot of talk about him then, but mostly I just listened because I didn't have much to say except I'd like to skin him alive."

"Then perhaps you *should* be suspected."

"Yeah, go ahead. The sheriff did a little."

"Why did he stop?"

"Because Harvey was just as good as me or better, and he's got it in for Harvey. And Harvey was out alone that afternoon, and I wasn't. Emmett Lake was with me right through, and Pete Ingalls too part of the time. The sheriff knew Emmett wouldn't lie for me because he thinks he ought to have my job."

"Balls," Emmett said.

He was ignored. Wolfe asked Mel, "You knew Brodell was back?"

"Yeah, we all did. We heard about it, Pete did and told us, the day after he came, a Tuesday. After supper that night the three of us had a big argument. Pete said we ought to offer to help Harvey and Carol keep an eye on Alma day and night to keep her from seeing him again, and Emmett said we ought to lay off because he might marry her, and I said it was up to her father and mother and we had to just leave it to them unless they asked us. Like every argument I ever had a part of, nobody changed anybody. But Harvey didn't say anything in the morning and neither did Carol, and it was a working day for all of us, and after supper Pete went off somewhere, and Emmett had a bellyache and went to bed. I told Archie all this."

"I know you did. The argument was resumed Wednesday evening?"

"Some. We had calmed down a little and we didn't work up a sweat. Thursday too, we had calmed down even more. Harvey had told me that Carol was sure that Alma hadn't seen him and wasn't going to. But like I told Archie, Pete and I were talking about him Thursday after supper, out by the big corral, right at the time he was laying on that boulder with two holes through him. It showed me once more, when I heard about it Friday, that you don't always know what you're talking about."

"How could you? Not only ignorance. Man's brain, enlarged fortuitously, invented words in an ambitious effort to learn how to think, only to have them usurped by his emotions. But we still try. Please continue."

Mel shook his head. "There's nowhere to continue to. I know what you're aiming at, you want to make it that somebody else shot that Brodell, not Harvey. I'd like that as much as you and Archie would, but if you want to brand a calf that's hid in the brush, first you've got to find him and tie him. What about that Haight kid?"

"Mr. Goodwin has eliminated him."

"No dice, Mel," I said. "I spent the morning on him, and he's absolutely out."

"Who's in?"

"Nobody. That's why we're here. Mr. Wolfe thought you might have heard something about Brodell that would point."

"I've been too busy to hear anything much, with Harvey gone. I've been across the creek just once in these two weeks, to Timberburg to see Harvey, and Morley Haight wouldn't let me. By God, I wish you could brand *him*."

Wolfe's eyes had gone right. "Mr. Lake. Tell me about Mr. Brodell."

"Dang Brodell," Emmett said.

Actually that isn't what he said. But about a year ago I got a four-page letter from a woman in Wichita, Kansas, saying that she had read all of my reports and that as each of her fourteen grandchildren reached his or her twelfth birthday she gave him or her copies of three of them just to get them started. If I go ahead and report what Emmett Lake actually said I would almost certainly lose that nice old lady, and what about the grandchildren who aren't twelve yet? I don't like censorship any better than you do, and if the payoff was going to be that it was Emmett who shot Brodell, I would have to report him straight and kiss Wichita good-by. But he just happened to be around because it was a ranch and he was a cowhand, so I'll edit him. Those of you who like the kind of words he liked can stick them in yourselves, and don't skimp.

"Dang [AG] Brodell," he didn't say.

"It can't be done," Pete Ingalls said. "He's dead and buried."

"It was me that said the atrocious [AG] scourge [AG] might marry her, and that shows what a misguided [AG] ignoramus [AG] I was."

"I thought you were showing understanding and compassion," Pete said.

"Balls. I said how I figured it. You know what I said. You're a lot younger than I am and you're bigger and stronger, but if I sit here and cross my legs good, let's see you get them opened up. Every breathing [AG] female [AG] alive is a born siren [AG]. The reason I called him an atrocious [AG] scourge [AG] was because he didn't belong here and all the panting [AG] dudes can thumping [AG] well leave their outstanding [AG] bats [AG] at home when they . . ."

Oh piffle [AG], that's enough. Censorship is too much work. I couldn't leave him out because he was there, but that will have to do for him. Wolfe stood it a little longer—he can stand anything if there's any chance it will help—and then stopped him by saying in a tone that had stopped better men with better vocabularies, "Thank you, Mr. Lake, for illustrating so well what I said about words. Mr. Ingalls. You have demonstrated that you have a supply of words too, less colorful. Mr. Goodwin has told me that you traded much more than twenty of them with Mr. Brodell."

"Last year," Pete said. "I didn't see him this year. I presume Archie has told you I agree with him on Harvey, but I've got a better reason. Harvey won't kill a fellow creature unless he intends to eat it. He doesn't even take shots at coyotes. The first year I was here, a horse broke a leg and had to be shot, and Harvey couldn't do it, and Mel had to. Now a man with an established psychological pattern like that, he might kill a man on a sudden irresistible impulse, but to suppose he would deliberately take a rifle and go hunting for a man and gun him down, that's just ridiculous. I know enough about—"

"If you please." Wolfe's tone wasn't the one he had stopped Emmett with, but it served. "Mr. Greve needs a liberator, not an advocate. You were with Mr. Brodell frequently last summer?"

Pete turned both palms up. He had a wide assortment of gestures. "I wouldn't say *with*. It's not the same thing, being *with* a man and merely being where he is. He was impressed by me, he sought me out, because he knew my father is a successful businessman—he's in real estate—and I'm doing advanced work in paleontology, and Brodell wanted to know how I broke loose. That was his phrase, 'break loose.' He wanted to break loose from his father and his newspaper, and his father wouldn't let him."

"What did he want to do?"

"Nothing."

"Nonsense. Only a saint wants to do nothing."

Pete grinned. "Man, that's good. I like that. It's not true, but I like it. Who said it?"

"I did."

"But who said it first?"

"I seldom let another man speak for me, and when I do I name him."

"I'll look it up, and if I find it I'll send you a crow to eat. But I take it back about Brodell wanting to do nothing. I should have said his one strong push was negative. I think a

lot of people are in that pinch; there's something they want
not to do so intensely that they can't take time to consider
what they do want to do. As for Brodell, I more or less
avoided him. I mean, when he wanted to arrange a double
date for us with a couple of girls in Timberburg I declined
with thanks. Things like that. Actually I saw very little of
him except Saturday nights at Woody's—once or twice I
ran across him at Vawter's, or he ran across me—and once
four of us spent an evening at a bowling alley in Timberburg. *De mortuis nil nisi bonum,* but he was dull. A very
dull man. I had a thought about him the day after he died:
I doubt if he ever stirred anybody. He was thirty-five years
old. It took him perhaps one minute to die, or even less,
but he probably stirred more people, he caused more ex-
citement, in that one minute of dying than in all his thirty-
five years of living. That's a dismal thought either about
life or about him. I figured it. There are eighteen million,
three hundred and ninety-six thousand minutes in thirty-
five years. You told us to talk about Philip Brodell and his
death. Well, if I tried all day I couldn't say anything truer
about him than that. That's a hell of an obituary."

"And surely not deserved," Wolfe said. "He must have
stirred Miss Greve. Unless you say, as Mr. Lake would, that
she stirred him."

"It's a point." Pete pursed his lips to consider it. "But it's
just semantics. 'Stirred.' Shall we debate it, does a girl have
to be stirred before she'll let a man take her? Of course not.
Some of them are, but only a minority; most of them let the
apron up because they've been curious about it so long. I
wish I knew Alma well enough to ask her. I don't believe
she was stirred. She had built up a good defense against
being stirred, but curiosity is often so strong that no man or
woman can resist it. Working with fossils, I have had the

thought that probably back in the Devonian, or even in the Silurian— Hi, Alma."

She had opened a door and stepped in. Four of us stood up. The custom of standing up when a female enters is hanging on longer in Montana than in Manhattan, and of course when Mel and Emmett did, Pete and I did too. Wolfe did not. He almost never does when a woman enters his office, and he had broken so many rules in the past three days that it must have given him real satisfaction to be able to stick to one. He had been introduced to Alma, and to Carol and Flora, when we arrived.

"Come and get it," Alma said, "before the grease sets." She had probably heard that summons to a meal before she grew teeth.

Mel went to wash his hands and the rest of us went to the dining room, which had been added on at Carol's request when Lily had had things done to the house. There was plenty of room at the long table; there were times when as many as four or five extra men had to be fed. Wolfe was put between Carol and Alma, and I was across from him and had a good view of his reaction to the tomato soup out of a can. He got it down all right, all of it, and the only thing noticeable was noticed only by me: that he carefully did not permit me to catch his eye. Flora was with us, between Mel and Emmett, and she helped Carol and Alma take out the soup plates and bring in dishes of mashed potatoes, string beans, and creamed onions. Then the real Montana trout deal, served by Carol and Alma from big trays. The longest and biggest foil bundle went to Wolfe. I had told him you didn't transfer it onto your plate; you just opened it up and pitched in. Which he did, after the women had sat and started theirs. His was a fine fish, a fat fifteen-inch rainbow Lily had caught, which she had shown me with pride, and I hoped it was cooked through. He used his knife and fork on it expertly, conveyed a bite to his mouth, chewed, swallowed, and said, "Remarkable."

That settled it; I would have to hit him for a raise. If redeeming me was worth *that,* I was being underpaid.

IX

NERO WOLFE SAID to Woodrow Stepanian, "No. After full consideration I might agree with you. I meant only what I said, that a majority of your fellow citizens would not."

It was twenty minutes to nine. We were in the middle section of the Hall of Culture, called the Gallery by Lily. The doors to the sections you had to pay to enter were both closed; the movie wasn't over and the romp hadn't started. Only one fact of importance had been acquired at the Bar JR: that trout baked in foil with ham, brown sugar, onions, and Worcestershire sauce was digestible. If we had got one from Mel or Emmett or Pete I didn't know it. I had got one from Saul Panzer, when I had called him on the Greves' phone. If Philip Brodell, on his visits to New York, had ever run into Diana Kadany or Wade Worthy, Saul had found no trace of it and thought the chance that there was one to be found was slim.

What Wolfe was saying he might agree with was something Woody had said regarding one of the items hanging on the wall back of Woody's desk—a big card in a home-made frame which said in homemade lettering by Woody:

> "ALL RIGHT, THEN, I'LL GO TO HELL"
> Huckleberry Finn
> by Mark Twain

Wolfe had asked why that had been chosen for display in a frame and Woody had said because he thought it was the greatest sentence in American literature. Wolfe had asked why he thought that, and Woody had replied because it said the most important thing about America, that no man had to let anybody else decide things for him, and what made it such a wonderful sentence was that it wasn't a man who said it, it was a boy who had never read any books, and that showed that he was born with it because he was American.

I had an errand to do, but I stayed to listen because I thought I might learn something either about America or about literature. When Wolfe said that a majority of Woody's fellow citizens wouldn't agree with him Woody asked him what they would regard as a greater sentence, and Wolfe said, "I could suggest a dozen or more, but the most likely one is also displayed on your wall." He pointed to the framed Declaration of Independence. " 'All men are created equal.' "

Woody nodded. "Of course that's great, but it's a lie. With all respect. It's a good lie for a good purpose, but it's a lie."

"Not in that context. As a biological premise it would be worse than a lie, it would be absurd, but as a weapon in a mortal combat it was potent and true. It was meant not to convince but to confound." Wolfe pointed again. "What's that?"

"That" was another hand-lettered item in a frame, but I can't show it to you because I didn't have a camera with me. Apparently it was eight or nine words, but what kind? The two words below, smaller, were "Stephen Orbelian."

"That is older," Woody said. "About seven hundred years old. I'm not sure it is great, but I have much affection for it because it is very subtle. It was written by that man, Stephen Orbelian, in ancient classical Armenian, and it says simply, 'I love my country because it is mine.' But of course it is not simple at all. It is *very* subtle. It means more different things than you would think possible for only eight words. With all respect, may I ask if you agree?"

Wolfe grunted. "I agree that it's subtle. Extraordinary. Let's sit and discuss it."

I wasn't invited to help, so I left to do the errand, which was merely a chauffeuring chore, driving the station wagon to the cabin to supply transportation for Lily and Diana and Wade Worthy. My expectation was that Lily and Wade would be in the big room, ready, but Diana wouldn't, and that was how I found it. Of course nine women out of ten are late leavers and arrivers, but with Diana it wasn't only that. She had to make entrances. She never just came to the kitchen at breakfast time; she entered. Without an audience, an entrance is merely an arrival, and the bigger the audience the better. The arrangement had been that I would come for them a little after nine. If Diana had been dressed and her face-work done at nine o'clock, she would have waited in her room until she heard the car, and in the hall until she heard me inside. So I was there telling Lily and Wade that the real Montana trout deal had gone down fine when Diana glided in, a treat for any audience in a red silky thing that started late at the top but nearly made it to her ankles at the bottom. Lily, who didn't sneer at audiences but had different ideas, was in a pale pink shirt and white slacks.

Back at Lame Horse there was no parking room left in front, so I circled around Vawter's to a secluded spot by the rear platform of the store, and we walked to the front through the passage between the two buildings. When we entered I wasn't expecting Wolfe to be visible. We had asked Woody for permission to use his living quarters in the back, and he had given it, with all respect, and the arrangement was that I would escort Sam Peacock there whenever I found, or made, an opportunity. But there he was, on a chair about half wide enough, by the rear wall, and he had company. The law was never much in evidence at the Hall of Culture's Saturday nights because the precautions Woody took never let anyone get out of hand. Now and then a uniformed state cop would drop in for a look, and that was all. But that evening not only was Sheriff Morley Haight there, on a chair some three steps to the right of Wolfe, but also one of his deputies, a well-weathered specimen with the kind of shoulders Haight wished he had, whose name was Ed Welch. He was standing over near the door at the right, where the man with the till was posted. Diana and Wade headed for that door, but Lily, beside me, looked at the deputy, then at the sheriff, and asked me, loud enough for him to hear, "Haven't I seen that man somewhere?"

To save me the trouble of providing a fitting reply she made for the door, taking her purse from her slacks pocket. I crossed to Wolfe and asked him, "Have you met Sheriff Haight?"

"No," he said.

"That's him." I pointed noticeably. "Do you want to?"

"No."

I turned to Haight. "Good evening. Do you want to ask Mr. Wolfe or me something? Or tell us something?"

"No," he said.

Thinking that was enough noes for a while, I went and handed the man at the door two bucks and passed through. The musicians were taking a rest, but as I was winding through the mob across to where I knew Lily would be, they started up, something I couldn't name, and Lily came to meet me, and we were off. Also on. We had moved together so many hours to so many beats that on a dance floor we were practically a four-legged animal.

We don't usually talk much while we're dancing, but in a minute she said, "He followed you in."

"Who? Haight?"

"No, the other one."

"I supposed he would. I didn't want to please him by looking back."

After another minute: "What does that ape think he's doing, sitting there?"

"Hoping. Hoping for an excuse to bounce us out of his county."

After another minute, during which we saw Diana hopping with a guy in a purple shirt and Levi's, and Wade with a girl in a sweater and a mini: "You said he was going to be in Woody's rooms."

"So did he. Evidently he decided to watch the herd arrive and spot the murderer. He is capable of deciding absolutely anything."

After two more minutes: "What is it about Sam Peacock? No, I take it back. I will *not* ask questions. It's just that seeing him sitting there, if it goes on much longer he'll decide I have to be obliterated, and damn it, he's the only man on earth I could be afraid of. Do you want to tell me about Sam Peacock or not?"

"Not. It may get us a lead, but don't hold your breath. As for Nero Wolfe, forget it. This will do him good. He even ate some of Carol's mashed potatoes. You didn't involve him and neither did I; he involved himself, and he's fully aware of it. He's aware of everything."

"I haven't seen Sam Peacock."

"He's always late. Last week he didn't come until nearly eleven. I told you, remember, I heard him tell a girl that when he was a yearling they had to tie his mother up before she'd let him suck."

When the band stopped for breath I took Lily to her favorite spot by an open window and went on a tour to see who was there, and to confer with myself. Deputy Sheriff Ed Welch was standing over by the band platform and I passed by with my elbow missing his by half an inch to show him how nonchalant I was. If Morley Haight was going to stay put on that chair in the Gallery, and he probably would when Wolfe went inside, I didn't like the program. Seeing me take Sam Peacock in to Wolfe, Haight would of course sit tight and collar Sam when he came out, and Sam was the one and only person from whom Wolfe might pry something to bite on. Not just his trying to slide past the Thursday morning when Brodell had gone for a look at Berry Creek; there was also all day Tuesday and all day Wednesday, when Brodell had been with him and no one else. And if Wolfe got a hint from Sam and Sam knew it, Haight would worm it out of him. I did not like the prospect that if we got a glimmer Haight would get it too, and I knew Wolfe wouldn't. As I moseyed past the door I took a look through at the Gallery. Haight was there, at Woody's desk, with a paperback, and Wolfe wasn't.

Moving around, and standing near a corner when the band was going, in the next half-hour I saw maybe 183 faces I had seen before, and I had names for about half of them, including most of the people you have met—everybody at Farnham's, and Pete Ingalls and Emmett Lake at the Bar JR. Pete was dancing with Lily, and she wiggled a finger at me as they went by. No Sam Peacock, but I saw a friend of his, the girl who had told him the week before that he looked awful. She had on the same cherry-colored shirt, or one just like it. When the band stopped and she walked away from her partner, looking as if she hadn't enjoyed it much, I went and headed her off and said, "I dance better than he does."

"I know you do," she said, "I've seen you. You're Archie Goodwin."

At close quarters she looked younger and prettier. Some do. "If you know my name," I said, "I ought to know yours."

"Peggy Truett. Thank you for telling me how good you dance. Now I know."

"That was just coiling the rope. The next move is to show you. I was leading up to it."

"I bet you were." She brushed back a strand of wavy blond hair. "You're shy, that's your trouble, I know. I'm not. Sure, I'd like to accept your kind invitation, but I guess I won't. I've seen you here a lot of times, last year and this year, and maybe you saw me, but you never headed in to me before, so why now? That's easy. You want to ask me about Sam Peacock."

"Do I? What about him?"

"You know damn well what about him. You and that fatty Nero Wolfe, last night you pumped him good just because he wrangled that dude and that was his job. If I was him I wouldn't give you—"

Her eyes left me, went past me, for something in my rear, and then all of her left. As she brushed my arm going by I turned for a look and saw Sam Peacock arriving. He saw Peggy Truett coming and came to meet her, and I looked at my wrist and saw that in nine minutes it would be eleven o'clock. The band started up and I moved to the wall, over near the door, and stood noticing pairings on the floor with my eyes only—Lily and Woody, Bill Farnham and Mrs. Amory, Pete Ingalls and Diana Kadany, Armand DuBois and a woman in a black dress, Wade Worthy and a girl from an upriver ranch. Ed Welch, the deputy, was sitting on the edge of the platform, a little higher than on a chair.

I was as useless there as a bridle without a bit, and I went out to the Gallery. Sheriff Haight was still there, with his feet up on Woody's desk, with a magazine. He had a glance for me but no words, and I had none for him. I stepped across for a look at the greatest sentence in American literature, which put me an arm's length from him, counted to a hun-

dred, and turned around. Yes. The deputy was there. I
thought of three different remarks to make to him, all witty,
vetoed all of them, crossed to the door at the back, opened
it and passed through, and shut it.

I was in Woody's kitchen, which was fully as modern as
the one at the cabin, though much smaller. Next came the
bedroom and bath, also small and functional, and then the
room that Lily called the Museum. It was big, about 24 by
36, with six windows, and it contained one or more speci-
mens of nearly every item Woody's father had peddled.
Name it and Woody would show it—anything from eight
different brands of chewing tobacco, plug and twist, in a
glass case, to an assortment of lace curtains on a rack. The
heaviest item was a 26-inch grindstone, not mounted, and
the biggest one was a combination churn and ice-cream
freezer. About the only things in the room that didn't qualify
were the chairs and the lights and the shelves of books,
which were all in hard covers. No paperbacks; it was
Woody's personal library.

When I entered, two of the books were on a small table
by the wall and one was in the hands of Nero Wolfe, who
was in a big, roomy chair by the table. At his left was a reading lamp and at his right, on the table with the other two
books, were a glass and two beer bottles, one empty and one
half full. He was so well fixed that I should have about-faced
and beat it, but he looked up and said, "Indeed."

Meaning where the hell have you been. So I moved a
chair to face him, sat, and said, "I told you he would be late.
He just came."

"You have spoken with him?"

"No. I doubt if I should."

"Why? Is he drunk?"

"No. But I have a case to put. Haight is still there and
shows no sign of leaving. So I get Sam, now or later, and

bring him, and in an hour, or six hours, either you get something or you don't. If you don't, you've wasted a lot of time and energy, which would be regrettable but that often happens. If you do, and when Sam leaves Haight is still there, what will happen will be worse than regrettable. Haight will—"

"I am not obtuse, Archie." He closed the book with a finger in at his place.

"I concede that."

"Isn't that"—he aimed a thumb—"an outside door?"

"Yes. I'm not obtuse either. I suppose you saw the brawny baboon who was standing there when I came, and you may have noticed that he followed me inside. That's a deputy sheriff, Ed Welch. I'm his subject for the evening. If I ushered Sam Peacock out the front entrance and around to the back, to that door, he would be close behind, and Haight would be even keener to work on him when he left. Of course leaving by that door wouldn't help; Welch would be out there waiting for him. I'm not sure we weren't both a little obtuse, especially me. I might have known Haight would be here. I should have hunted Sam up this afternoon, or even at suppertime, instead of that goddam real Montana trout deal. So all you have to show for tonight is a trout recipe which you will of course pass on to Fritz, and a subtle sentence in ancient classical Armenian. Tomorrow is Sunday and Sam will probably have a day off, but I'll find him and bring him. The more I look at it, the more I like Sam Peacock. I do not believe that Brodell had no suspicion that there was someone in the neighborhood who would like to get him, and I also do not believe that during all of Tuesday and all of Wednesday, and part of Thursday, he didn't say a single word that would provide a hint. Didn't I say that, or something like it, three days ago?"

"Not three. Two. Thursday afternoon. You said you had

tried to use what you called my 'filter job' on him, and he wouldn't cooperate."

"He certainly wouldn't. You got more out of him last night than I had in three tries. But now it's you, not just me, and you're official, and he knows it. I suggest that we now leave by the back door and I drive you to where your bed is so you can get a night's sleep, and tomorrow I'll bring him. I'll come back for the others."

He made a face. "What time is it?" he growled.

I looked. "Twenty-four minutes to midnight."

"I'm in the middle of an exposition that is refreshing my memory." He poured beer and opened the book. "Perhaps you should tell Miss Rowan we are going."

I said it wasn't necessary, that we usually stayed until around one o'clock, and went to look over his shoulder to see what was refreshing his memory. It was a volume of Macaulay's *Essays,* and he was on Sir William Temple, of whom I had no memory to be refreshed. I moved around, with my eyes and sometimes my hands on museum pieces, but my mind was on people, specifically Morley Haight and Ed Welch. I was not admiring them. If a sheriff and his top deputy are so strong on law and order that they stay on the job Saturday night, they could find better things to do than try to trip up a pair of worthy citizens who had been authorized by the county attorney to investigate a crime in their territory. They needed to have their noses pushed in, and I considered three or four possible ways of taking a stab at it when I got back, but none of them was good enough.

It was close to midnight when Wolfe finished the beer, closed the book, switched the lamp off, picked up the other two books, went to return them to their places on the shelves, and asked me, "The glass and bottles?" At home, at that time of night, he would have taken them to the kitchen himself, but this was far away and called for allowances, and

I made them and obliged. When I returned from the kitchen he was in another chair, bending over to turn a corner of a rug up for inspection. He knew a lot about rugs and I could guess what he was thinking, but he didn't even grunt. He put the corner down and got up, and I went and opened the back door, which had a Murdock lock, and he came. He asked if we should turn the lights out and I said no, I would when I returned.

Outside, a little light from the draped windows helped some for the first twenty yards, but when we turned the corner of the deepest wing of Vawter's it was good and dark, with no moon and most of the stars behind clouds.

We took it easy on the rough ground. No other car had joined the station wagon there in back of the building. I had taken the ignition key but hadn't locked the doors, and, leading the way, and regarding it as common courtesy, not pampering, to open the door for Wolfe on his side, I did so. That gave us light, the ceiling light, and the light gave us news. Bad news. We both saw it through the closed window. On the rear seat. Rather, partly on the seat. His torso was on the seat, but his head was hanging over the edge and so was most of his legs.

Wolfe looked at me and took a step so I could open the door. I didn't want to touch the damn door or anything else, but it was possible that he was breathing, even in that position, so I pressed the latch and pulled it open and leaned in. The best quick test is to lay something light and fluffy on the nostrils, but nothing that would do was handy and I reached for a wrist. No perceptible pulse, but that proved only that if the blood was moving it was dawdling. The wrist was warm, but of course it would be since I had seen him on the dance floor only an hour ago. The only blood in sight was some blobs on his bruised ear, and I stretched across to get fingertips on his skull and felt a deep dent. I backed

out and stood and said, "It's barely possible he's alive. I stay
here and you go in. You'll have to tell that sheriff sonofa-
bitch, and that's a lousy break too. Tell him to bring a doctor, there are at least two there." I reached in the front to
the dash and got the flashlight, switched it on, and focused
it on the entrance to the passage between the buildings.
"That's the shortest way. Here." I offered him the flashlight
but he didn't take it. He spoke.

"Wouldn't it be possible to—"

"You know damn well it wouldn't. There's one chance in
a million he's alive, and if so he may talk again. You don't
have to tell him it's Sam Peacock, just say a man. Here."

He took the flashlight and went.

X

THE HUMAN MIND is a jumbo joke, at least mine is. There were a dozen or more urgent questions it could have been considering as Wolfe disappeared in the passage, but what it was asking was, how will Lily get home? I had that answered, fairly satisfactorily, and was deciding what to work on next when I heard footsteps in the passage. It was Haight, with a flashlight, presumably Lily's. He came, looked in at the news, turned to me, and asked, "Is this your car?"

He couldn't have asked a dumber question if he had tried all night. How could it be my car if I didn't have one and he knew it? "You'll find the registration card," I said, "in the dash compartment. Is a doctor coming?"

"Get in the front seat," he said, "and stay there." He transferred the flashlight to his left hand and aimed it at my eyes and put his right hand on the butt of the gun at his belt.

"I prefer," I said, "not to touch any part of the car. If I wanted to blow I probably wouldn't have waited here for you. I'm pretty sharp in an emergency. Is a doctor coming?"

"I ordered you to get in the front seat." He pulled the gun out.

"Go climb a mountain, with all respect."

It was a relevant question, was he actually dumb enough to think I might scoot or jump him, or was he just being J. Edgar Hoover? I haven't answered it definitely, even yet, because it got complicated by the sound of stumbling feet in the passage, and Haight pointed the flashlight that way as a baldheaded man in a loud plaid sports jacket came into view. It was Frank Milhaus, M.D., whom I knew by sight but had not met. He stopped at the rear end of the station wagon and looked around, and Haight said, "In the car, Frank," and he came and looked in. He turned to Haight and asked, "What happened to him?"

"*You* tell *me*," Haight said.

By stooping and putting his right foot in and his left knee on the seat, Milhaus got his eyes and hands where they could see and feel. In three minutes he came back out and said, "His head was hit hard at least three times. I think he's gone, but I can't be sure until—here he comes."

It was Ed Welch, with a flashlight in one hand and something black in the other. He came and looked at the object in the station wagon and said, "That's Sam Peacock." For the lowdown on anything, you couldn't beat the law officers of Monroe County. Milhaus took the black thing, a doctor's kit case, put it on the front seat, opened it, took out a stethoscope, and again maneuvered in to what had now been officially identified as Sam Peacock. In a couple of minutes he came out again, said, "He's dead," and started folding the stethoscope tubes.

"That's final?" Haight asked.

"Of course it's final. Death is always final."

"Anything besides the blows on the head?"

"I don't know." He put the stethoscope in the case, shut it, and picked it up. "He's dead, evidently by violence, and I'm not the coroner."

"We'll get him out where you can look him over."

"Not me. As you know, I've had a run-in that I don't care to repeat."

He started off. Haight said something to his back, but he kept going, to the passage, and was gone. Haight turned to me and said, "You're under arrest. Get in the front seat."

"Charged with what?" I asked.

"Held for questioning will do for now. Material witness. Get in the front seat."

"You're in the saddle," I said. "For now. But every inch of this car is going to be—"

I stopped because of the kind of movement Ed Welch made with his shoulder as he took a step toward me. It meant what it usually means. His right fist came around for my jaw, not a jab or a hook, but in orbit. By the time it got there my jaw was some six inches to the rear, and it went on by. But Haight was moving too, to my right, with his gun out, and he poked it in my ribs, the lower ones. Welch was starting another swing, and when it came I did a fancy job of dodging; I turned my head just enough so that it connected, but on a slant. It wouldn't have toppled a window dummy, but I staggered, lost my balance, and went down flat on the ground.

Welch kicked me, probably aiming for my head, but there wasn't enough light and it got my shoulder. I don't like to report what he said because you probably won't believe it, but it's a fact and I'll include it. He said, "Resisting arrest." With no one to hear him but Haight and me. I sent my eyes right and left into the darkness, thinking there might be an audience he had wanted to impress, but no. Then he said, "Get up, you."

I stayed flat on the ground for the same reason that I had gone down, because I knew what would happen if I stayed on my feet. Perhaps I haven't made it clear enough, the mood I was in after those two weeks of fizzles, and then Wolfe coming, and then Gil Haight out. And now Sam Peacock gone. The edge I was on was just too damn thin. If I had stayed upright, either I would have put both Welch and Haight on the ground, and don't think I couldn't, or I would have got a bullet or bullets in me. So there I was with a sharp pebble under my hip and a bigger one under my shoulder.

Welch said, very rude, "Goddam you, get up."

I thought he was going to kick me again and so did he, but Haight said, "He's pissed his pants. If Milhaus leaks there'll soon be a mob out here. Go in and send Farnham out, and Evers if you find him quick, and phone Doc Hutchins to come and come fast. The body's not supposed to be moved until he sees it, for Christ's sake."

I know exactly how long I stayed down. Forty-two minutes, from 12:46 to 1:28. I like to keep track of important events. As far as Haight and Welch were concerned I could have been up much earlier, since they soon had all they could do with the arrivals from three directions—through the passage and around the corners of Vawter's and the Hall of Culture. Whether the word had been started by Dr. Milhaus, who obviously had no love for Haight, or by Farnham or even Welch himself, here they came, and for half an hour I had a good worm's-eye view of Haight waving his gun and squawking, and Welch shoving, and Bill Farnham trying to guard both sides of the station wagon at once. At that, they did the job. The only man who got close enough to the car to touch it was Dr. Hutchins, the coroner, who arrived at 1:19. By that time Haight had recruited three or four men to lend a hand with the crowd, and two more to bring their cars for illumination from their headlights, and things were pretty well under control. At 1:28 Haight was standing just four steps from me, talking with Dr. Hutchins, and I thought I might as well see if he was still set on getting me into the front seat, and got to my feet. I leaned over to brush my slacks off, and when I straightened up Ed Welch was there. His right hand wasn't a fist; it couldn't be because it held a pair of handcuffs. His left hand started for my right one, but missed it because I extended both of mine, to give him no excuse for wrist-twisting, and he snapped the cuffs on. They were one of the newer models, nice and shiny.

"My car's out front," he said. He pointed to the passage. "That way." He gripped my arm.

The crowd may have thinned a little, but there were more than a hundred pairs of eyes to watch their officer of the law escort his prisoner, obviously dangerous since he was man-acled, away from the scene of the crime. I used my pair of eyes too, and as we neared the end of the passage I saw her, Lily, standing at the edge of the beam from one of the head-lights. Diana and Wade and Peet Ingalls were with her. They waved to me, and I waved back—with both hands, of course —and Lily called, "Woody took him." That was a relief. I had been half expecting that when we got to the car Wolfe would be in it, also handcuffed, and that would be too high a price even for me.

But there was someone in the car, a Mercury sedan, dou-ble-parked in front of Vawter's. It was Gil Haight, in the driver's seat. As Welch opened the rear door Gil swiveled his head around on his long neck, and as I climbed in I said distinctly, "Nice mahrnin'," and Gil laughed. Not a mean laugh, just a nervous laugh. Welch got in beside me and pulled the door shut and said, "Okay, Gil, roll. Your dad said to tell you to come right back."

It was a quarter past two when we pulled up at the curb in front of the courthouse in Timberburg, and nobody had said a word. When three men ride that many bumps and curves together and no one speaks there's a bad circuit some-where, and on that occasion probably two—between Welch and me, and between Gil and Welch. When Welch and I were out and the door shut, he said, "Tell your dad I'll be right here," and Gil said, "Yeah." Four teen-agers, two male and two female, passing by, stopped to look when they saw I was handcuffed, so Welch had an audience again as he took me to the steps and up to the entrance. In the big lobby he steered me to the side hall at the right, and along it, and when we got to the door I had entered sixteen hours earlier, *not* handcuffed, he stopped, got a ring of keys from a pocket, and used one. That surprised me because I had supposed that by that time someone would be on post in the sheriff's office to channel communications. Welch flipped the wall switch for light, motioned me through the gate in the railing and to a chair at the end of a desk, and sat at the desk.

He asked me a loaded question: "Your pants dry yet?" Since it was loaded I ignored it. He opened a drawer, took out a pad of printed forms, wrote on it at the top with a ball-point pen—presumably the date and hour—and asked me two factual questions: "Your name's Archie Goodwin? A-R-C-H-I-E?"

"I want to phone my lawyer," I said.

He grinned at me. He meant it to be a mean grin, and it was. "Every Friday night," he said, "Luther Dawson goes to his cabin up in the hills south of Helena. There's no phone and—"

"Not Dawson. I want to phone Thomas R. Jessup."

That erased the grin. "Jessup's not your lawyer," he said.

"He's *a* lawyer. I have a paper in my pocket signed by him. I'm willing to change my request. Demand. I want to telephone a lawyer."

"I'll tell the sheriff when I see him. A-R-C-H-I-E?"

"Just put an X. You probably don't know what 'stand mute' means, but I do. Also you may think that a man can't stand mute while he's sitting down, but he can. It's a trick. I answer no questions about anything until I see Mr. Jessup, not even important ones. Ask me which I prefer for breakfast, ham or bacon, and I'll stand mute. But you haven't asked me, so I'll just mention that the best way is to bring

me both and I'll take my pick. Or even better, to prevent
waste . . ."

I was prattling on because he was trying to think, and with
me talking it might be not merely difficult for him but im-
possible. Of course his problem wasn't me, really; it was a
man whose name he could spell without asking, Thomas R.
Jessup. He would probably have liked to consult Haight, but
the sheriff was reachable only on Woody's phone if at all.
When he finally got it thought through, and picked up a
phone and pushed a button, I expected him to dial Woody's
number, but he didn't touch the dial. In a minute he spoke:

"Mort? Ed Welch. I've got one for you here in the sheriff's office. Come and get him. . . . No, he can walk. . . .
What the hell do you care? Come and get him." He hung up
and started writing on the pad.

I looked at the gate in the railing and considered ways and
means. There weren't any. Lily was certainly trying to get
Dawson, and Wolfe was probably trying to get Jessup, but
all I could do about that was to wish them more luck than
they were likely to have. It was more than likely, it was next
to certain, that I would not only have neither ham nor bacon
for Sunday breakfast; I wouldn't even get them Monday.
The question was, could I do anything about anything?
Could I, for instance, say something to Welch that might
have some effect on how *he* spent the rest of the weekend?
I had got nowhere with it when the door opened and Mort
appeared. He was a wiry little guy with a long red scar on
his left cheek, in gray uniform pants with a permanent
crease, and a dirty gray shirt, and a gun in his belt. Welch
looked at him and demanded, "Where's your jacket?"

"It's hot in there," Mort said. "Just overlook it."

"I ought to report it." Welch rose, got his key ring from
a pocket and selected one, and came and unlocked the cuffs

and took them. "Stand up," he said, "and empty your pockets. Everything."

As I rose I said, "I'll keep the paper signed by Thomas R. Jessup."

"You'll keep nothing. Unload."

I obeyed. I made a pile on the desk, glad that there was nothing strictly private like a copy of the letter I had written Wolfe. When I had finished, Welch went over me and did a good job, not too rough, and then he handed me a surprise. When he picked up my wallet and took the bills out I supposed he was going to count it and have me sign a slip, but he didn't even flip the edges. He held them out and said, "You can keep this," and when I took it he picked up the chicken-feed and handed me that too. That had never happened to me before in any of the coops I had been checked in at, and it was an interesting new item for my file of Montana folkways. Of course it could be only local; there could be someone inside, an inmate or one of the help, who had fast fingers and split his take with the front office. It isn't reasonable to expect the people who run a jail to average up any better than those who run things on the outside.

Welch told Mort, "Put him in five and don't get in front of him. Is Greve still in twelve?"

Mort nodded. "You know he is."

"All right, put this one in five. Evers can get his prints later. It looks like he's a killer and you may have him a long time. I can't give you his name on the record because he's not talking, not even his name. Call him whatever—"

"I know his name. Goodman." Mort put his hand on his gun. "On out, Goodman. Turn right."

I obeyed.

XI

At ten minutes past five Sunday afternoon a turnkey inserted a key in the lock of my cell door and turned it, opened the door, and said, "Someone for you."

I did not respond with enthusiasm. It couldn't possibly be Wolfe or Lily. Conceivably it was Luther Dawson, since Lily could be extremely energetic when she wanted to, but if so it would be only a courtesy call. One of the bets I had made with myself during the day was 20 to 1 that no judge would be available on an August Sunday for setting bail. It might be Sheriff Haight, but that would be no treat. He would merely try to get me to talk and I would merely try to think of bright remarks about standing mute. So I wasn't bothering to guess as I crossed to the door, which took two and a half steps.

It was Ed Welch, and I raised a brow when I saw he had handcuffs. That must mean a trip, and to where? He snapped them on, jerked his head to the right, and said, "Take a walk," and I headed down the corridor. Passing the door with the figure 12 on it I hoped Harvey wouldn't look out and see me, since I couldn't stop and explain how I got there. Welch used a key on a big barred door at the end of the corridor, and another one at the far side of the square room, and we were at the end of the side hall of the courthouse. So it would be the sheriff's office, and probably the sheriff. But it wasn't. We went on by to the big lobby, across to the main stairs, and on up. I began to think I might have been wrong about judges, Lily and Dawson might have scared one up, but at the top of the stairs Welch steered me to the right and on to a door I had entered before. It was standing open, and a man appeared on the sill as we approached—the man whose name was on the door, County Attorney Thomas R. Jessup. We were still four paces away when he spoke.

"Why the handcuffs, Welch?"

"Why not?" Welch asked.

"Take them off."

"If that's an order, it's your responsibility. He resisted arrest."

"It's an order. Take them off and take them with you. I'll ring you when—"

"I'm not leaving. I have orders to stay with him."

Jessup took a step into the hall. "Take off those handcuffs or give me the key. If you don't know what the boundaries of authority are, Sheriff Haight does and I do. Don't enter my office. I'll ring you when to come for him. Give me the key."

Welch had to do some more thinking. But it took him only a few seconds to decide he needed help on it, and the nearest help was downstairs. He got his key ring out, removed one of the keys, handed it to Jessup, and turned and marched off. It was a good performance. Better men than him, including me, have had trouble getting a key off of a ring, and he had done it, smooth and fast, under pressure.

Jessup motioned me in, followed, and shut the door. He was about as slim and trim as usual from the neck down, but his eyes were red and the lids puffed and he hadn't shaved. There were a desk and a table in that room, but no one was at them, and there was no one in the inner room he ushered me to. There was good light from the three windows, and he looked at me and said, "I don't see any marks."

"None anywhere," I said, "except maybe my shoulder where Welch kicked me. I resisted arrest by ducking when he swung a wide one." I put my hands out, and as he used the key on the handcuffs and slipped them off he asked, "How much have you talked?"

"Not at all, except telling Welch what 'stand mute' means and saying I wanted to phone a lawyer named Jessup. That was around three o'clock this morning. Since then there has been no one to talk to."

"Haight?"

"No sign of him."

"Well, you'll do some talking now, but first—" He pointed to a carton with cord around it on a chair. "That's from Miss Rowan. A snack, she said. Do you want to eat first or talk first?"

I said I would rather get the talking done and take my time with the eating, and he went to his chair behind his desk. As I took one across from him he got an envelope from his breast pocket. "This explains itself," he said, and offered it, and I reached to take it. It wasn't sealed, and it held a single sheet of paper, Lily's Bar JR letterhead, and the writing on it, in a hand I knew, said:

AG: I have spoken at length with Mr. Jessup and have reserved nothing relevant to the inquiry we are engaged on. Therefore neither will you. We are committed with him irrevocably, and I think he is with us.

August 11, 1968   NW

I folded it and put it in the envelope and stretched across to hand it back to Jessup. "I'd like to have it later," I said, "as a souvenir, but Welch will frisk me again when he gets me back. Okay, I talk, but first a couple of questions. Where is Mr. Wolfe?"

"At Miss Rowan's cabin. I have certified in writing that he

is under arrest, that his movements are under my control, and that he is not to be molested without reference to me. The legal force of that document is questionable, but it will probably serve. Your other question?"

"What dented Sam Peacock's skull?"

"A rock not much bigger than your fist. He was hit with it four or five times. It was found there on the ground about twenty feet from the car. Dr. Hutchins is sending it to the laboratory at Helena, but from his own examination he is certain it is the weapon. He says its surface is too rough for fingerprints. It could have been picked up anywhere. As you know, that's rocky ground."

"Has anybody got any ideas? Any you've heard about?"

"No. Except about you, of course. You were there, and you know how that is. In that note Wolfe says that you are irrevocably committed with me, and he thinks I am with you, and he's right. I'm stuck with you, and I hope to God I don't spend the rest of my life regretting it. After my talk with Wolfe I am completely satisfied that you didn't kill Sam Peacock, but that doesn't help much. It doesn't help at all with the squeeze I'm in. Wolfe thinks the two murders are connected, Brodell and Peacock, and I suppose you do."

"Certainly. Any odds you name, you've got a bet."

"Why?"

"I'll get to that." I leaned back and crossed my legs. The chair was a big improvement on the stool in my cell. "Naturally you want to compare what I say with what Mr. Wolfe said. Starting where?"

"The day he came. If it's more than I want, I'll tell you."

I talked. It required no special effort, since I was to reserve nothing relevant. The only point that needed consideration, as I went along, was whether this or that detail belonged in, and I gave most of them the benefit of the doubt and included them. One that I omitted was the phone calls to Saul

Panzer; he was two thousand miles from Jessup's jurisdiction. For the conversations, I gave him summaries of all of them except Wolfe's with Sam Peacock Friday evening; I reported that verbatim. He was a good listener and interrupted with questions only twice, and he took no notes at all. I ended with the last two relevant conversations, mine with Peggy Truett on the dance floor and mine with Wolfe in the Museum.

"Then," I said, "we went out to the car and opened the door, and there it was. I doubt if you need or want what happened next, since it's relevant to me but not to the inquiry. I'm getting hoarse because my throat's dry. The room service downstairs is none too good. Is there water handy?"

"I'm sorry. I apologize. I should have—" He was out of his chair. "Scotch or rye?"

I said just water would do but scotch would be welcome if it wanted in, and he went to a copper-colored refrigerator in a corner and took things out. A woman would have found only one flaw: he didn't use a tray. I found none. When he returned to his chair there was on the desk in front of me a man-sized glass containing two ice cubes immersed in whisky, and a pitcher of water, and he had a glass too. I filled mine to the top, put the pitcher in his reach, took a healthy sip, and cleared my throat.

"That helps," I said, and took another sip. "Now connecting the two murders. Of course the first point is that Mr. Wolfe and I *want* them to be connected, but there are other points. There at Farnham's Friday evening Mr. Wolfe let them all hear him concentrate on Sam Peacock, and he made it obvious that he was by no means through with him. It could be that one of them knew that Sam had seen or heard something that Mr. Wolfe must not know about, but it doesn't have to be. All of Farnham's crowd were there last night, and one of them may have told somebody how Nero

Wolfe had concentrated on Sam." I took a swallow and put the glass down. "The shortest way to say what I'm saying is to repeat what Mr. Wolfe once told a man: 'In a world of cause and effect, all coincidences are suspect.' There were more than two hundred people there last night, maybe three hundred, and one of them was murdered, and which one was it? It was the man who had been alone with Brodell the two days before *he* was murdered and who was going to be worked on by an expert. I not only suspect that coincidence, I reject it."

Jessup nodded. "So does Wolfe."

"Sure. He thinks things through like me. Did my report match his fairly well?"

"Not fairly. Perfectly."

"He has a good memory. This drink has reminded me that I'm hungry. When I smelled the Sunday dinner downstairs I decided to fast. Mr. Wolfe never talks business during a meal, but I do." I rose. "May I open that carton?"

He said certainly, and I went and got it and put it on the desk. The knot looked complicated, and I borrowed his knife to cut the cord, opened the flaps, and unpacked. When I finished there was an imposing spread lined up on the desk:

> 1 can pineapple
> 1 can purple plums
> 10 (or more) large paper napkins
> 8 paper plates
> 1 jar caviar
> 1 quart milk
> 8 slices Mrs. Barnes's bread
> 6 bananas
> 1 plastic container potato salad
> 4 deviled eggs
> 2 chicken second joints
> 1 slab Wisconsin cheese

1 jar pâté de foie gras truffé
1 huckleberry pie
6 paper cups
2 knives
2 forks
4 spoons
1 opener combo
1 salt shaker

I said I hoped he was hungry too, and he said he had told Miss Rowan that he would also have me brought on Monday, if circumstances permitted.

"Of course," he said, "there will be people coming and going tomorrow and it would be a little complicated. Miss Rowan tried all morning to get Luther Dawson but couldn't reach him. He's not accessible weekends. He may not get to his office before noon tomorrow but Miss Rowan has his home telephone number, and it's about a three-hour drive here from Helena. But there will be a judge available tomorrow at any hour. You realize that my position is a little —well, difficult. In a court proceeding in this county I represent the people of the State of Montana, and Haight will insist that I ask for high bail. He may even want me to ask that you be held without bail, but of course I won't. I have explained the situation to Wolfe and Miss Rowan."

My mouth was busy with deviled egg. I had the caviar jar open and was working on the pâté. I swallowed. "It's not the being in that hurts," I said, "it's the not being out. After being completely useless for two weeks, I could now do some detective work with a real chance of ringing the bell if I wasn't locked up." I slid some of the items toward him. "Help yourself to something. Everything."

"Thanks." He reached for a slice of bread and the caviar. "What would you do if you were out?"

"What Haight should be doing but probably isn't—and

Welch too, instead of chaperoning me. Do you want me to describe it?"

"Yes."

I spread caviar on bread. "I have it all in order after the hours I've spent looking at it. How did they get out there back of Vawter's—Peacock and X? They arranged to meet there. In advance? No. After Peacock arrived, at nine minutes to eleven. They spoke, there on the dance floor, and arranged to meet outside. They left separately, not together, and—"

"That's merely assumptions."

"Certainly. That's all you ever have to start, assumptions. You assume the probables and file the possibles for later if they're needed. So three things happened there on the dance floor: Peacock and X spoke, and X left, and Peacock left. People saw those three things happen. Find those people. That's what I would be doing if I were loose. It's a kindergarten chore, but most detective work is. I said it's what Haight should be doing, but actually, if he keeps his eyes open when he's on duty, he shouldn't have to. If he stayed where he was when I went in to Mr. Wolfe at a quarter past eleven, and that's another probable, he was right there, not ten steps away from the door they left by. The reason I assume they left separately, I certainly assume that when X left he did not intend that Peacock would be coming back. He had probably already been out there behind Vawter's for a look, and he may have had the rock in his hand when Peacock came. But those are just details to help pass the time when you're sitting on a stool in a cell. The question is, who was seen talking with Peacock on the dance floor? And who left the dance floor between eleven-fifteen and midnight?" I knifed a gob of pâté onto a piece of bread and, having finished the whisky, poured milk.

Jessup was forking a second joint to a paper plate. "But," he objected, "many people leave, don't they?"

"I wouldn't say many. Sure, some go out and most of them come back in, but that doesn't queer it, it merely complicates it. May I have a sheet of paper and a pen or pencil? Anything—that scratch pad."

He handed me the pad and a pen from his pocket. I chewed bread and pâté and drank milk, which was warm, while deciding how to put it, and then wrote:

NW: I am talking to and with Jessup, as instructed. I'm glad you're under house arrest because this jail is old and they use too much disinfectant. I suggest that you have Miss Rowan or someone at the ranch find and bring a girl named Peggy Truett. She was a friend of Peacock's and she probably knows things. She may even know who Peacock went out to meet. I hope Haight doesn't get to her before you get her to you. I also hope I won't have to go to St. Louis because now you have stirred him and we should get him right here.   AG   8/11/69

I handed it to Jessup and said, "Read it, and the sooner he gets it the better."

He read it, and then read it again. "Why this? Why not phone him?"

I shook my head. "That line may be tapped. From what I have been told about Haight and his feelings about you, it could even be that *yours* is tapped."

"It's a hell of a situation, Goodwin."

"I agree."

He looked at the sheet. " 'Now you have stirred him.' Stirred him how?"

"My God, that's obvious. Of course Peacock might have got killed anyway—for instance, if he was on a blackmail caper and overplayed it—but maybe not. He would probably still be alive if Mr. Wolfe hadn't started in on him. Of course Haight should have done that long ago, or you should."

He ignored the dig in *his* ribs. "Peggy Truett is the girl you were talking with when Peacock arrived."

"Right. I reserved nothing relevant. If you prefer to get at her yourself I suppose it's—"

"I don't." He looked at the sheet again. "You won't have to go to St. Louis. A man named Saul Panzer is going. In fact"—he looked at his watch—"he's there now if his plane was on time."

"Oh." I finished spreading an ample layer of caviar on a full slice of bread. "I don't think I mentioned him, but evidently Mr. Wolfe did. He called him? When?"

"This morning. I drove him to Woody's. He told Panzer to put another man on the job in New York—I forget his name—"

"Orrie Cather, probably."

"That's it. And he told Panzer to take the first available plane to St. Louis and gave him instructions. I think Wolfe has decided—no, not decided, assumed—that one of the persons at Farnham's had a previous connection with Brodell. We went there when we returned from Woody's—Wolfe and Miss Rowan and I—and I asked them to allow Miss Rowan to take pictures of them. With her camera. I know nothing about cameras, but apparently she does."

I nodded. "She knows enough. Did any of them object?"

"No. Farnham didn't like it, but of course he wouldn't. She seemed quite expert. I brought the film and a man I know is developing it. I intended to take the prints to Miss Rowan later this evening, but with your message for Wolfe I'll go now. Or as soon as the prints are ready. I like Miss Rowan's conception of a snack. She seems to be aware that man cannot live by bread alone. She is leaving early in the morning for Helena to get the prints off to Panzer by air mail and to get Luther Dawson. She is not— You'll remember that at our previous encounter she ordered me to leave."

"She suggested that you go and sit in the car. This is good cheese. Have some."

"And if I didn't you would drag me. That episode is now forgotten by mutual consent. I'm going to repeat to you a confession that I made to her. Not for quotation. I think I funked it. I should have realized long ago that the conflict between Haight and me could be resolved only by the destruction, the political destruction, of one of us, and I should have seized the opportunity offered by his inefficient investigation of the murder of Philip Brodell. I said I'm stuck with you and Wolfe, and I'm glad I am. If we lose, it will finish me, but I don't think we will." He took some cheese.

"Did you say that to Mr. Wolfe?"

"No. I said it to Miss Rowan. His manner is . . . he doesn't invite . . ."

"I know. I have known him quite a while. That's a good way to put it, he doesn't invite. Tell him and Miss Rowan that since they're doing so well without me they don't need to bother about bail, they might as well save the expense, and anyway I don't like Dawson. Haight will probably turn me loose when they deliver X to him. Is there room in that refrigerator for what's left?"

"Certainly. But there will be people here all day."

"Wait until they're gone. I probably won't be hungry sooner anyhow. That disinfected cell doesn't seem to whet a man's appetite." I picked up the can opener. "Plums, or pineapple?"

XII

I NEVER GOT around to asking, so I still don't know what happened to the rest of that snack.

The next time you're in jail, try this. There are two steps. The first step is to determine whether there is anything helpful and practical that you can be using your mind for. If there is, okay, go ahead and use it. If there isn't, proceed with the second step. Decide definitely and positively to cut all connections between your mind and you. I understand that something like that is used by people who are trying to go to sleep and can't make it, but I don't know how well it works because I never have that problem. Locked in a 6 by 9 cell and wide awake, you'll be surprised at how the time will go. You will find, if you are anything like me, that your mind knows a thousand tricks and can sneak in through a crack that you didn't even know was there. For instance, at one point that Monday afternoon, having another try at it, I decided to shut my eyes and look at girls' and women's knees, having learned hours ago that you have no chance at all unless you make your eyes see something or your ears hear something or your fingers touch something; and in a cell you have to see or hear or touch things that aren't there. So I looked at dozens, maybe hundreds, of females' knees, all shapes and sizes and conditions, and was in control and doing fine when all of a sudden I realized that my mind had plugged in and was asking me if I thought that anyone was at that moment looking at Peggy Truett's knees, and if so

was it Nero Wolfe or Sheriff Haight . . . and what were
they saying. . . .

Nuts. I got up and kicked the stool clear to the far wall,
at least three feet, and walked to the end wall, at least four
feet, and reached to feel the rusty bars at the doll-size window. I knew them by heart.

I am not going to report on the food because you would
think I'm prejudiced. I honestly believe they put disinfectant
in the oatmeal and the stew.

When footsteps stopped at my door at twenty minutes
to six I was lying on the cot with my shoes off, wondering
if Jessup still had company in his office. I admit the remains
of the snack were a factor, but I was hungrier for news than
for grub. The footsteps stopping was nothing; he often
stopped to look in to see if I was sawing the bars or making
a bomb, but when I heard the key in the lock I moved. I
swung my legs around and sat up. The door opened and a
man entered and said, "You're takin' a walk. Get your shoes
on and bring your coat."

It was Evers, the other full-time deputy. He stood and
watched me put my shoes on, and my jacket, and when he
told me not to leave anything and stooped to look under the
cot I knew I wasn't going upstairs, I was going out and not
coming back. He didn't have handcuffs, and on the way down
the corridor, and then down the side hall of the courthouse,
he didn't care whether I was in front or behind. He opened
the door of the sheriff's office and thumbed me in. There
was no one in the anteroom, and he opened the gate in the
railing and jerked his head and said, "On in." I crossed to
the door to the inner room and entered, and he followed.

Haight was there at his desk, busy with papers. The eminent lawyer who looked more like a working ranchman,
Luther Dawson, was standing with his back to Haight, looking at a big wall map of Montana. At sight of me he came

with a hand out and a hearty welcome. "Well, greetings!" He had a good grip. "I come to deliver you from bondage. All signed and sealed."

"Fine. Next time I'll pick a better day than Saturday." I pointed. "I believe that's mine." It was a pile of objects on a table. I went and retrieved my possessions, with Evers at my elbow. Everything was there, including the contents of the card case, which belongs in my breast pocket, and the non-negotiable items in the wallet, which goes in my pants pocket. As I picked up the last item, the ignition key of the station wagon, Evers said, "Sign this," put a sheet of paper on the table, and offered a pen.

Dawson said, "Let me see it," and stuck a hand between Evers and me to take it.

"No matter what it says," I said, "I don't sign it. I sign nothing."

Dawson asked, "Were you given a receipt for those things when they took them? An itemized receipt?"

"No, and even if I was, I sign nothing." I headed for the exit. I didn't give Haight even a glance, but I have good side vision, and the corner of my eye noted that he was too busy with the papers to look up. Probably Wyatt Earp. There were footsteps behind me, presumably Dawson's, and out in the hall he came abreast and said, "Miss Rowan's out in front. In a car. I have something to say, Goodwin."

I stopped and faced him. Our eyes were exactly on a level. "Not to me," I said. "Ten days ago today, on Friday, August second, I told you that I thought a man named Sam Peacock might know something that would help, but he had clammed up on me, and probably a famous Montana lawyer like you could pry him loose. And you said you were too busy with important matters. Now nobody is going—"

"I didn't say that. I said only—"

"I know what you said. Now nobody is going to pry him

loose. And Harvey Greve didn't kill *him*. So that's another important matter. Have you talked with Nero Wolfe?"

"No. He refuses to see me. I intend to—"

"I don't give a damn what you intend, but if my name is in your script anywhere, cross it out. I had to shake hands with you in there because there were witnesses." I moved.

I thought that should make it clear that I wanted to be alone to enjoy my liberty, and it did. Going down the hall I heard no footsteps behind me. There were a few people scattered around in the big lobby and I heard someone say, "There's that Archie Goodwin," but I didn't stop to take a bow. On the walk outside I sent my eyes left and right but didn't see Lily until the second try because she was half a block away, in a dark blue Dodge Coronet sedan. Her attention was on something down the street in the other direction, and she heard me before she saw me. I opened the car door and said, "You don't look a day older, let alone two days."

She squinted at me. "You do."

"I'm two years older. Are there any errands for us?"

"No. Get in."

She was in front but not behind the wheel. "You'd better move to the back," I said. "And open both windows. I don't smell, I stink. I doubt if you can stand it."

"I'll breathe through my mouth. Let's go."

I circled around to the other side, got in, started the engine, backed out, and headed east. I asked if the car was a rental, and she said yes, the sheriff had the station wagon, and anyway she didn't want it. She didn't want a car a man had been killed in.

"I couldn't ask Dawson what my price tag is," I said, "because I was dressing him down. How much?"

"Does it matter?"

"It does to me. For the record. The lowest so far was five

hundred, and the highest thirty grand. What am I worth to the people of the State of Montana?"

"Ten thousand dollars. Dawson said five thousand and Jessup said fifteen and the judge split the difference. They didn't ask me."

"What would you have made it?"

"Fifty million."

"That's the way to talk." I patted her knee.

We were in the open country. For a mile or so I played on the gas pedal to test the engine, and it was okay. Lily asked, "Aren't you going to ask me any questions?"

"Yeah, plenty, but not between bumps. There's a spot not far ahead."

It was just beyond a gully, where the road went north for a stretch, with a stand of lodgepole on the left. I slowed and eased off of the blacktop into the shade the trees gave from the slanting sun, stopped, killed the engine, and twisted around to face her. "For two days and a night," I said, "I've been wanting to ask people certain questions, and this is my first chance, so I'll start with you. When I left the dance floor Saturday night about a quarter past eleven, soon after Sam Peacock arrived, you were dancing with Woody, Farnham had Mrs. Amory, DuBois had a woman in a black dress, and Wade had a girl I had seen before but can't name. Did you see Peacock at all?"

"I saw him twice from a distance. Later I looked around but didn't see him, and I didn't see you either. I supposed you had taken him in to Nero Wolfe."

"I hadn't. With Haight and Welch there, we decided to skip it. Now this is important. After you danced with Woody, did you see Peacock talking with anyone you know?"

"No." She frowned. "I only saw him from a distance, and I don't . . . No."

"Did you see anyone you know leave the dance floor? Go out to the Gallery?"

"If I did, I didn't notice. No."

"As I said, it's important. It's crucial. As you know, people often see something and don't know they're seeing it. If you'll sit down, or lie down is better, and shut your eyes, and go over everything you saw and did, starting from when you were dancing with Woody, you might come up with something. Will you give it a try?"

"I doubt—but I'll try, of course."

"Okay. Now some things that you *are* aware of, but first a word of stomach-felt appreciation. You don't like to give or receive thanks for things that should be taken for granted, and neither do I, but there's a limit. *Six* bananas. A *whole* pie. The best caviar *and* the best pâté. And calling it a snack was false modesty deluxe. But you saved my life."

"Go to hell, Escamillo. I got you into this."

"You did not. X did, and he's going to regret it. Now. Where is Mr. Wolfe?"

"I think at Woody's. We'll stop there. Yesterday and today he has spent more time at Woody's, and at the ranch, than he has at the cabin."

"Why the ranch?"

"Because that girl's there. Peggy Truett. Carol got her last night—she lives in Timberburg—and brought her to the cabin. Jessup was there, and they questioned her for more than two hours. In your room. Around eleven o'clock Jessup came to the big room and phoned Carol and told her they were coming with Peggy Truett. They went in Jessup's car. It was after midnight when he brought Wolfe back. They told me nothing, not a damn thing, and this morning I left for Helena before seven o'clock. With this car. I haven't been back, but about two hours ago I called Carol, and she said Wolfe had been there nearly all day talking with Peggy

Truett, and he was still there, and he had asked her if she would drive him to Woody's around five o'clock. So I think he's at Woody's but he may still be at the ranch. You know him better than I do. Peggy Truett may be his type."

"He hasn't got a type. It's a filter job."

"What's that?"

"It's similar to what I asked you to do about Saturday night, only he steps it up by asking questions. It's the opposite of filtering coffee. With coffee you're after what goes right through, but with her he's after what doesn't go through, or doesn't want to. Then you don't know whether Haight has seen him or not."

"No. Does that matter?"

"Probably not. Only if those two have conversed I have missed something I would have enjoyed. Let's see, what else? Oh. Jessup said you went to Farnham's and took pictures, and that nobody objected but Farnham, but of course he would. Did anybody want to object but decided not to? I assume you were aware that you were pinch-hitting for me."

"Of course. You might have seen signs that I missed. Jessup made it an official request, but he explained that it *was* a request and anyone who wanted to could refuse without giving a reason. Very neat, I thought. You and the genius are making a man of him. Sitting still like this I do seem to notice a slight—uh—aroma. Kind of exotic. Will it go?"

"No, it's permanent. Our future contacts will have to be outdoors in a strong wind. You sent the prints to Saul?"

"*Did* I. I was up and dressed at six o'clock, and I got them on the ten-o'clock plane. He should have them by now. You think it was one of them, don't you?"

"I don't think anything. I have no right to think until I earn it by doing a little work." I started the engine and moved the pointer to D. "And take a bath." We bumped back onto the blacktop.

It was ten minutes to seven when we rolled to a stop in front of the Hall of Culture and I climbed out and crossed to the screen door and entered. There was no one in the Gallery, but the door at the rear, to the kitchen, was standing open, and I went and stuck my head in. Woody was on a stool at the counter, stirring something in a bowl, and Wolfe was standing at his elbow, watching. With Wolfe in it, the kitchen looked smaller than it was. I stepped in and said, "Just in time."

Wolfe looked at me, took a step for a closer look, and growled, "Satisfactory."

My nerves were a little raw. "What's so damn satisfactory about it?" I demanded.

"You're here, you're intact, and you have your tongue. 'Just in time.' Yes, you are. You are just in time for Mr. Stepanian's favorite dish, *hunkiav beyandi*. He says it was originally Armenian, but the Turks have claimed it for centuries. It's kebab served with eggplant stuffed with a purée which the Turks call *Imam Baïldi—'Swooning Imam.'* Onions browned in oil, tomatoes, garlic, salt and pepper. Was that jail dirty?"

"Yes."

"Are you hungry?"

It was understandable that he didn't want to report with Woody there, and apparently there was nothing so urgent that it couldn't wait until he had tasted *hunkiav beyandi*.

"Certainly I'm hungry," I said, "but first I have to scrub, and Miss Rowan phoned Mimi to have some filets mignons out. She thought you might be hungry too."

"If you will excuse me," Woody said, "there is my tub and shower and plenty of hot water, and I would be honored.

You know how glad I am to see you, Archie. As Mr. Wolfe says, it is satisfactory."

"And I'm glad to see you, Woody." To Wolfe: "So I'll come back later. Around nine?"

He looked at the clock on the wall. Right at home. "I expect telephone calls. And I must make one. Nine or ten, any time. Or Mr. Stepanian can take me; he has kindly offered to. I suggest that you bathe and eat and go to bed."

"That's a wonderful idea," I said. "Gee, it's a good thing I stopped, I never would have thought of it. See you tomorrow. Good night, Woody." I turned and walked out.

As I opened the car door Lily said, "He's not coming?" but I waited until we were on the way to answer.

"Some day," I said, "I will brown him in oil and sprinkle garlic on him. He is expecting phone calls. He suggested that I bathe and eat and go to bed. So either he has got something hot started that he thinks he doesn't need my help with, or he is cooking up one of his screwy charades that he knows I wouldn't like. Listen to me. That shows the frame of mind I'm in. You don't cook a charade. Now as I lie and soak in a tub of water just hot enough, I won't be making careful plans for tomorrow; I'll be wondering what the hell we're in for. From now on ignore me. Pretend I'm not here. If there was a dog at the cabin to come bouncing to greet me, I'd kick it."

She said nothing for a mile, then: "I could go and borrow Bill Farnham's dog."

"Fine. Do that."

As we turned into the lane: "But you're going to eat."

"You're damn right I am. I'm starving."

The ignition-key routine at the cabin was not to bother about it in the daytime, but the last one using the car in the afternoon or evening was supposed to take it in and put it at a certain spot on a shelf in the big room. So I took it, to show Lily and whom it might concern, meaning me, that I was through with it for the night. If Woody reneged on his offer to drive Wolfe home, he could walk.

I ate. Clean as a scraped trout, shaved, shampooed, manicured, teeth brushed, clad in a handsome gray silk belted toga with black dots, over white pajamas with no dots, I sat in the kitchen with Lily and ate turtle soup, two filets mignons, hashed-brown potatoes, bread and butter, milk, spinach with mushrooms and Madeira, honeydew melon, and coffee. Twice Diana came and asked if she could get us anything and we said no thanks, and the third time, when Mimi was pouring coffee, she asked if she could have some and we said yes. As she sat she said she had been dying to ask me about being in jail, and so was Wade; and she called him and he came.

I told them about the jail, making it pretty damn grim, putting in some bugs that were apparently attracted by the disinfectant, and a couple of lizards. Then they asked about the finding of Sam Peacock's body, and then the big question, who killed him and why? On that, of course, I said that their guess was as good as mine, or better, since I had been in the clink; and I suggested a game of pinochle. I said a friendly game of pinochle would help to get my mind off of the ordeal I had been through. I did not say that it would be satisfactory, for me, to have Wolfe come and find me enjoying myself, with no concern for trivial things like murders; I merely thought it. Lily knew, of course; as we rose to go to the big room a corner of her mouth was up with that understanding smile that means, any woman to any man, *How well I know you.*

But I didn't get the satisfaction. Shortly after eleven o'clock sounds came: a car stopping out in front, the car door slamming, the car moving again, faint footsteps, a door opening and closing, and footsteps in the long hall, receding.

We had been visible through the window, but he had gone
to the door to the hall and to his room.

"Nero the great," Wade said. "I'm not jeering, Archie, or
if I am it's not at his talents, only at his manners. If he doesn't
want to tell us about things he might at least take the trouble
to say good night to his hostess. And you. Does he even
know you're out of jail?"

I nodded. "Oh, sure. Lily and I stopped at Woody's and
he was there. He was watching Woody cook something the
Turks stole from the Armenians. Your deal, Diana." I was
entering the score. "If you'll deal me a two-hundred meld
we'll collect."

She did and we did, though I almost spoiled it by making
a dumb lead.

My decision to go and tell Wolfe good night was not a wag
of my tail. As I told Lily when Diana and Wade had gone to
their rooms, it was just possible that he had had a reason for
putting on an act with Woody there, and a broad-minded
man like me should give him a chance to say so. Therefore
I went down the long hall, quietly even on the tile in my soft
deerskin slippers, knocked on the door at the end, barely
heard the "Come in," and entered. He was in his yellow
pajamas, barefooted, in the chair by the window, which was
closed.

"I may sleep until noon," I said. "Good night."

"Pfui. Sit down."

"I need a lot of rest after—"

"Confound it, sit down!"

I went to a chair and sat.

"I assume," he said, "that Miss Rowan has told you that
Mrs. Greve brought that girl."

"Yes. And she took some pictures and sent them to Saul,
who is in St. Louis, and you and Jessup have been working
on Peggy Truett practically nonstop. I'm sorry I missed it."

"So am I. It should be a settled policy that all interviews with women are handled by you. Then you know that she is at the ranch. Mr. Jessup put her under arrest yesterday evening; the current euphemism is 'protective custody.' She is being protected from annoyance by Sheriff Haight, with Mrs. Greve and Miss Greve as her warders. She was and is an essential link. It's worthy of remark that although you were confined you supplied a name that made it possible to arrange for the denouement."

"I did?"

"Yes."

"It's arranged?"

"Yes."

"You've got it?"

"Yes. The last call from Saul, an hour ago, settled it, and I called Mr. Jessup to tell him. A man or men will arrive in Helena at nine tomorrow morning and proceed to Timberburg. I am stretching a point and telling you that. The circumstances do not permit that I tell you more at present."

My mouth opened and shut again. My eyes took him in, from the high and wide forehead down across the sea of yellow to the bare feet, and back up again. "If this is one of your spectacular razzle-dazzles," I said, "with a long and tricky fuse, and if you leave me out because I might refuse to play, and if it blows up in your face, you won't lose a client or a fee, you'll lose me, and after what you've gone through the last five days, that would be a shame."

"It would indeed." He shook his head. "It isn't that, Archie. You'll have to await the event. But I must consult you now on a detail. I observed that with the other car there was a key which had to be turned to make it start, as with my cars which you drive, and the key was not left in the car overnight. It was brought inside and placed on a shelf. Is there a similar key with the car Miss Rowan has now?"

Naturally I suspected him of changing the subject just to sidetrack me, but I said only, "Yes."

"And the car can't be started without it?"

"It *can* be, but you have to have a couple of tools and you have to know how. I could do it, but you couldn't."

"I couldn't even with the key, and certainly wouldn't. Is the key for Miss Rowan's car on the shelf now?"

"It should be. I put it there."

"Get it in the morning, before breakfast, and put it in your pocket. I could do that myself, but it would be awkward if Miss Rowan wanted to use the car. That's the detail. It's late. Good night."

There was no point, absolutely none, in wasting my breath on either a comment or a question, and I was tired all over. I rose, said good night, and went. By the time I got to my room I had decided that either Wade Worthy or Diana Kadany was it, and by the time I was under the blanket with the light out I had decided it was Wade because I couldn't see Diana smashing Sam Peacock's skull with a rock.

XIII

AT FIVE MINUTES PAST NINE Tuesday morning I concluded that it couldn't be either Wade or Diana.

The conclusion was on good and sufficient grounds. As you know, having murder suspects for fellow guests had been hard for Wolfe to take, and if one of them was no longer merely a possible candidate, if the denouement he had arranged for was to put the tag on one of them, he certainly wouldn't show up for a sociable breakfast, even if it meant going without. But when I entered the kitchen, with the car key in my pocket, there he was, seated across from Wade, drinking orange juice, talking man to man. Mimi was at the range turning French toast, Lily was arranging bacon on a platter, and Diana was pouring coffee. As I exchanged good mornings and joined Wolfe and Wade at the table I was not in a mood to be the life of the party. It was nice to know that I wouldn't be eating breakfast with a murderer, but in that case why did I have that car key in my pocket?

The answer came with the second batch of French toast. The conversation had been mostly about jails, which apparently had a fascination for Diana. Wolfe was telling about one in Austria he had once escaped from, and he turned to Lily and said, "Speaking of escape, Miss Rowan, it would be ungracious to regard my departure from here as an escape, but I didn't come for pleasure, and I won't pretend that I shall be sorry to get back to my proper milieu. Mr. Goodwin and I will be leaving soon, probably tomorrow morning. Your hospitality and your tolerance of my temperament have been the mitigation."

Lily was gawking at him, and she is not a gawker. She looked at me, saw nothing helpful, and looked at him. "You say . . ." She returned to me. "You're going too, Archie?"

I don't know what I would have said, with the other two guests there, if Wolfe hadn't fielded it. "It's barely possible," he said, "that the event will not meet my expectation, but I don't think so. I spoke on the telephone yesterday, several times, with a man in St. Louis—a man named Saul Panzer, whom I sent there—and there seems to be no doubt. Mr. Panzer had photographs of people who are now in Montana, and one of them has been identified by several people in St. Louis. Six years ago, in the summer of nineteen sixty-two, a young woman met a violent death. She was strangled, throttled with a man's belt. The belt and other evidence pointed to a man named Carl Yaeger as the probable culprit, but he wasn't apprehended because he couldn't be found. He had decamped. He has never been found—until now. One of the photographs Mr. Panzer had was of Carl Yaeger, and a St. Louis policeman is now on his way to Montana. Indeed—what time is it, Archie?"

"Nine-thirty-seven."

"Then he arrived at Helena half an hour ago and is now en route to Timberburg." He focused on Lily. "So it is reasonable to suppose that my expectation will be realized. I don't give you the man's name—the name you know him by—because of my semi-official status. My commitment to Mr. Jessup. But I can tell you that certain evidence indicates that Carl Yaeger is remarkably versatile in method. He strangled a woman, shot a man, and crushed another man's skull with a rock. Not many murderers have so patly fitted the crime to the occasion. So Mr. Greve will soon be released, probably in time for Mr. Goodwin and me to greet him before we leave."

Lily was squinting at him. "Then you—you really—"

"We really have brought it off. Yes. I tell you now because I would like to exchange favors with you. I need some trout. I know there are more and larger trout in the river, but there are some in the creek, and the size I prefer. If you and Miss Kadany and Mimi will take the day for it you can reasonably expect to be back by five o'clock with enough for my purpose. Can't you?"

Lily was still squinting. "That depends on your purpose."

"That's my favor. Yours, for me, is to get the trout. Mine, for you, is to serve a real Nero Wolfe trout deal at your table. It can't be true *truite Montbarry* because some of the ingredients are not at hand, but I'll manage. If you will?"

Lily sent me a look that asked, "Is this part of a screwy charade that you don't like?" I answered out loud, "Of course if I went along we'd be sure of getting enough, but I may be needed to run an errand. Anyway, three of you—you only have to get five or six ten-inchers apiece."

I had had to change my conclusion again, the second time in less than an hour, since it was now obvious: I had the car key in my pocket because Wade Worthy was it and he had been tipped off. But what came next? Was Wolfe sending the females off to spare them the sight of one guest being forcibly detained by another guest? If so, why hadn't he waited until they were gone to raise the curtain? Those questions, and others like them, were in my mind as Wolfe finished his fifth or sixth piece of French toast, and Wade decided he had had enough toast and bacon but kept his hand steady as he lifted his coffee cup, and Lily and Diana and Mimi agreed that they had better leave by ten o'clock and take a can of salmon eggs just in case. I said Wade and I would clean up but was ignored, and as they started operations we left—Wade to the right, to his room, and Wolfe across to the outside door. I followed him out to the terrace and across it. Apparently he was going to the car to make sure the key wasn't there, but he went on by, nearly to the beginning of the lane, stopped, and said, "We're out of earshot."

"Yeah. We're also out of step. I wait until Miss Rowan is even further out of earshot and then show him my credentials and take him? Is that it?"

"No. If it were, I would have told you beforehand. There is nothing for you to do, or me either, until Mr. Haight comes for him, with the St. Louis policeman. That will probably be around one o'clock. The St. Louis man will get to Timberburg about noon, and according to Mr. Jessup he will go to the sheriff's office. That's the normal procedure. And Mr. Haight will bring him here."

I was staring at him. "And meanwhile, I do *not* take Carl Yaeger alias Wade Worthy?"

"Yes. You do not. I presume he will not be here when they arrive. How and where he will have gone, I don't know. Finding that the key to Miss Rowan's car is not available, he will probably cross the creek and go to the ranch, hoping to take one of the cars there, but Mrs. Greve and Mr. Fox will have made sure that he can't. Therefore he will have to walk—or run—presumably to Lame Horse. Stop staring at me. If I don't tell you the details of the arrangement you'll probably go dashing off in pursuit, so I had better tell you."

He told me.

XIV

THEY CAME AT ten minutes past one.

Wolfe and I were seated in the two best chairs on the terrace, discussing the character and career of Woodrow Stepanian. With the women gone, and Wade gone, we were as alone as if we had been in the old brownstone on West 35th Street. We hadn't seen Wade go, so he had probably crossed the creek for a try for a car at the ranch, as Wolfe had supposed. We had been very busy. I had put the clothes I had worn in jail out to air, draped on bushes, because there wouldn't be time to have them washed or cleaned. I had done a thorough job on Wade's room, not to get anything on or about him, but to collect and remove everything connected with the book he wasn't going to write. It filled two cartons, which I took to Lily's room. I took a look around her room, and mine, and the big room, to see if anything was missing, but that was just a professional gesture, since he had left on foot in a hurry and needed to travel light. I had phoned Med-Continent Airlines in Helena to reserve two seats on the morning flight to Denver and a connecting flight to New York. Wolfe had done four things: packed most of his belongings, inspected every shelf and cupboard in the storeroom, but not the freezers, to get ingredients for a real Nero Wolfe trout deal, read a chapter in the book about Indians, and made a casserole of eggs *boulangère* for our early lunch. Before joining him on the terrace I had locked the windows and outside doors of the cabin.

It was Haight's black Olds sedan that came down the lane and stopped right in the middle of the clearing. Three men climbed out—Haight, Ed Welch, and a six-foot square-jawed guy in a blue suit that looked as if it had been traveled in, which was to be expected if he had just arrived from St. Louis. All the attention Wolfe and I got was side glances. The stranger came and stood at the edge of the terrace, and Haight and Welch went and pushed the button at the cabin door. Getting no response, they knocked, twice, the second time good and loud. Haight pulled the screen door open and tried the knob of the solid one with no luck. He said something to Welch, and Welch went to the other door, to the hall, and tried that. He returned to Haight, and they both left the terrace at the right end and disappeared around the corner of Lily's room. The stranger turned and approached Wolfe and me, and spoke. "I'm Sergeant Schwartz of the St. Louis police. I believe you're Nero Wolfe."

Wolfe nodded. "I am. And Mr. Archie Goodwin. You may as well sit."

"Thank you very much. It's a pleasure, Mr. Goodwin." But he didn't sit; he stood and looked around at the scenery, and in a couple of minutes the other two appeared, at the left, having circled the house. Haight came and confronted me and demanded, "Where's Miss Rowan?"

I shook my head. "I'm out on bail. Standing mute."

"You goddam punk, where's Wade Worthy?"

I tapped my lips with a fingertip.

Wolfe said, "I'm articulate, Mr. Haight. But I like eyes at a level, so you'll have to sit down if you want to talk."

"Where's Wade Worthy?"

"Sit down or leave. All of you. This will take a while. Carl Yaeger, alias Wade Worthy, is not on the premises."

"Where is he?"

"Sit down or go."

Sergeant Schwartz was moving. He went to a chair facing Wolfe, sat, and asked politely, "Where is Carl Yaeger, Mr. Wolfe?"

"I don't know. I should mention that we were expecting you, Mr. Schwartz. I assume you have met Mr. Saul Panzer, whom I sent to St. Louis. Having spoken with him on the telephone late last evening, I knew you were coming."

Schwartz nodded. "I knew you knew. You don't know where Carl Yaeger is?"

"No."

"When did you see him last?"

"About four—" Wolfe stopped because of the noise made by the chairs Haight and Welch were shoving. When they were in them he said, "About four hours ago. But it—"

"Is he in the cabin?" Haight demanded.

"No. I said—"

"Why are the doors locked with you sitting out here?"

"To keep you from entering. There is no one inside. The keys are in Mr. Goodwin's pocket. We preferred not to let you invade Miss Rowan's house in her absence. I have important information for you, Mr. Haight, about Wade Worthy, but I'll supply it only in proper sequence without interruptions. If you won't take it that way you won't get it."

"The information I want, I want to know where he is."

"I'll get to that. But I'll start at the beginning. Nineteen days ago, in the morning of Thursday, July twenty-fifth, Philip Brodell went—"

"To hell with Philip Brodell! I want—"

"Shut up."

You would have to hear that particular tone of Wolfe's to appreciate it. I don't know how he does it. It wasn't anything like as loud as Haight's bark, but it cut through and stopped him.

"You'll hear this as I choose to tell it," Wolfe said, "or

not at all. That Thursday morning Philip Brodell went for a walk, alone, for a look at Berry Creek—as he told Sam Peacock. Reaching the creek, he continued downstream as far as this cabin—or, alternatively, Wade Worthy had gone upstream from the cabin. Which, isn't essential; the essential point is that Brodell saw Worthy and recognized him as Carl Yaeger, and Worthy knew it. They may have exchanged words, but that isn't essential either. Brodell returned from his walk, had lunch, and took a nap. The question, why didn't he telephone someone in St. Louis immediately to tell of his seeing Carl Yaeger, is one of many questions that will never be answered, since both Brodell and Peacock are dead. At three o'clock, encountering Sam Peacock as he left to go to Blue Grouse Ridge to pick huckleberries, Brodell told him that he had that morning seen a murderer. Precisely what he—"

"You can't prove any of this," Haight said. He had switched to Wyatt Earp. "Peacock's dead. I don't believe a word of it, and nobody else will."

Wolfe cocked his head at him. "Mr. Haight, you are the kind of man who has to be heard to be believed. If you had any gumption at all you would realize that I am prepared to show all my cards, and you would withhold comment until you see them. Precisely what Brodell told Peacock that Thursday afternoon is conjectural, as are many other collateral details—for instance, how Worthy contrived to see Brodell leave that afternoon, and trail him to Blue Grouse Ridge, without being seen by Peacock. But the requisites are established. It is established that Brodell told Peacock enough to cause him to suspect, when he found Brodell's body with two bullet holes in it, that Wade Worthy had fired the shots. For confirmation of that, that it's established, I refer you to Mr. Jessup, the county attorney. Information about

it has been acquired from a young woman whom he is holding in protective custody. I shall give—"

"Holding her where? What's her name?"

"Ask Mr. Jessup. I'll give you no particulars about her;
ask him. I'll tell you this: one point that is *not* established
is the use that Sam Peacock was trying to make of his information—or suspicion. The easy and obvious assumption
is blackmail, but the young woman denies it. There are other
possibilities. If he had only a suspicion, he may have been
harebrained enough to try to confirm it himself before di-
vulging it. Or he may have had a strong animus for Mr. Greve
and was reluctant to succor him. As for animus, should you
ask if I have any for you, I have indeed. A barely competent
inquiry into the death of Philip Brodell would have included
rigorous and repeated questioning of Sam Peacock, and if
it had it is highly probable that Mr. Goodwin would have
left long ago and I would never have come."

He turned a palm up. "But it didn't. As for Peacock,
whatever his objective was, he didn't reach it. He arranged,
or agreed, to meet with Worthy, Saturday evening, and he
died. Incidentally, it is likely that Worthy suggested that
they meet at or in that car. He had arrived in it, and he knew
it was secluded there, and dark."

Schwartz spoke. "You're saying that he killed two men."

Wolfe nodded. "And of course that isn't good news for
you. It isn't likely that Montana will let Missouri have him."

"Provided Montana has him or gets him. You say he's not
here. But you saw him four hours ago?"

"Yes. I ate breakfast with him. I had a personal problem.
I knew that you were coming, that you would go to the
sheriff, and that he would bring you here. For six days I
had been sharing Miss Rowan's hospitality with Mr. Worthy,
and Mr. Goodwin had been here with him much longer.
To cause her to suffer the indignity of having one of her

guests arrested on a charge of murder in her house, taken across her threshold in manacles, was of course unthinkable. For we were responsible; Mr. Goodwin and I had exposed him. It was necessary to use subterfuge, and I did. At the breakfast table, with him there, I announced that a photograph of a man now in Montana—I didn't name him—had been identified as one Carl Yaeger, who was wanted in St. Louis as a murder suspect, and that a policeman was coming for him. I then suggested to Miss Rowan that she and her other guest, and her maid, go fishing, and they did. It was desirable for her to be absent when you came."

All three of them were staring at him. It was Haight who demanded, "And where's Worthy?"

"I don't know. Mr. Goodwin and I came outside for a talk, and when we went back in a little later he was gone. Presumably he left by the back door and crossed the creek and—"

"Why, you goddam fat— *You'll* go in handcuffs! And Goodwin!"

"No, Mr. Haight. I have a suggestion. Mr. Goodwin will unlock the door, and you'll go in and telephone Mr. Jessup's office. He let me do it this way because he appreciated the contribution Mr. Goodwin and I have made. At his request, members of the state police were stationed at certain spots at nine o'clock this morning—I don't know how many, but certainly enough to make sure that Carl Yaeger, alias Wade Worthy, wouldn't get far. He is undoubtedly in custody now, probably at a police barracks, if they have them in Montana. Or Mr. Jessup may have him at his office. I suggest that you telephone."

XV

A REPORT SHOULD END with a flourish, but this one can't. The groan has nothing to do with murder or trout; the state cops delivered Yaeger-Worthy to Jessup's office safe and sound, and the fisherwomen came back a little after three o'clock with five cutthroats, two browns, four Dolly Vardens, and seven rainbows. For five of us, even though one was Nero Wolfe, that was ample.

The gloomy item left to report is the job I had to tackle, telling Lily that she would have to start all over again on the book. Find another writer and then start him from scratch. Awful. But since looking forward to a tough job is even worse than doing it, I didn't put it off. When the trout had been admired and turned over to Wolfe, and they had scattered to go and change, I went to my room and through the little hall, tapped on the door of Lily's room, was invited to enter, and did so. She was in a chair by a window running a comb through her hair.

"I have news," I said, "but you'll have to take the bad with the good. In one way it's—"

Nuts. Why should I annoy you with it? Let's have a flourish. Harvey Greve was turned loose in time to come and see Wolfe and me off for Helena in the morning.